YA
'ee
pb

FEElings on Trial

"I told Terry the three of us could go to the movie together on Wednesday and—"

Jake interrupted Nancy. "I can't believe it. You know I don't like Terry, for starters. Also, he's interested in you. So why would the *three* of us go anywhere together?"

Nancy looked stunned. "I didn't think it would be a problem. I mean, Terry knows that I'm your girlfriend."

"Does he?" Jake asked, growing hotter by the second. "He sure doesn't act that way."

"What do you think he's going to do—send you to buy popcorn so he can make a pass at me?" Nancy said.

"I wouldn't put it past him," Jake muttered under his breath.

NANCY DREW ON CAMPUS™

Available from ARCHWAY Paperbacks

For orders other than by individual consumers, Pocket Books grants a discount on the purchase of **10 or more** copies of single titles for special markets or premium use. For further details, please write to the Vice-President of Special Markets, Pocket Books, 1633 Broadway, New York, NY 10019-6785, 8th Floor.

For information on how individual consumers can place orders, please write to Mail Order Department, Simon & Schuster Inc., 200 Old Tappan Road, Old Tappan, NJ 07675.

Nancy Drew
on campus ™ #20

Jealous Feelings

Carolyn Keene

EAU CLAIRE DISTRICT LIBRARY

AN ARCHWAY PAPERBACK
Published by POCKET BOOKS
New York London Toronto Sydney Tokyo Singapore

T 110079

The sale of this book without its cover is unauthorized. If you purchased this book without a cover, you should be aware that it was reported to the publisher as "unsold and destroyed." Neither the author nor the publisher has received payment for the sale of this "stripped book."

This book is a work of fiction. Names, characters, places and incidents are products of the author's imagination or are used fictitiously. Any resemblance to actual events or locales or persons, living or dead, is entirely coincidental.

AN ARCHWAY PAPERBACK *Original*

An Archway Paperback published by
POCKET BOOKS, a division of Simon & Schuster Inc.
1230 Avenue of the Americas, New York, NY 10020

Copyright © 1997 by Simon & Schuster Inc.
Produced by Mega-Books, Inc.

All rights reserved, including the right to reproduce
this book or portions thereof in any form whatsoever.
For information address Pocket Books, 1230 Avenue
of the Americas, New York, NY 10020

ISBN: 0-671-00212-0

First Archway Paperback printing April 1997

10 9 8 7 6 5 4 3 2 1

NANCY DREW, AN ARCHWAY PAPERBACK and colophon
are registered trademarks of Simon & Schuster Inc.

NANCY DREW ON CAMPUS is a trademark of
Simon & Schuster Inc.

Cover photos by Pat Hill Studio

Printed in the U.S.A.

IL 8+

CHAPTER 1

"Come on, Drew. You're studying the history of Western civilization, not the history of Jake Collins."

Nancy Drew drained her coffee mug and tried to concentrate on her notes. She had a quiz in her Western civ class later that morning, but she was so tired she had decided to put in her last hour of studying at Java Joe's, a coffee bar on campus. But the coffee must not have hit her yet, because she wasn't absorbing anything. All she could think about was Jake.

After a great, relaxing weekend with her boyfriend, Nancy was having trouble getting in gear for the week ahead. Jake was a junior, and she'd met him at the college newspaper, where they were both reporters.

1

On Sunday they had taken a short road trip and spent the day wandering around flea markets and antique stores, and picnicking at a nearby orchard. It had been totally romantic being wrapped in Jake's arms and sharing grilled chicken and brownies and crisp tart apples. Nancy shivered as she remembered Jake's delicious kisses. They had been having problems lately, and for a while, Nancy had questioned her commitment to him. Now, though, everything seemed to be back on track between them.

Still, their troubles may have been worth the time they needed to work them out, Nancy decided, twirling her reddish blond hair around the pencil she was holding. Once she and Jake were alone now, they had nothing to argue about.

"You know, nothing goes better with coffee than a fresh croissant."

Nancy looked up from her notes. Terry Schneider was standing beside the table, his black canvas book bag slung over his shoulder. He held a giant mug and a croissant for himself.

"Actually, on Monday morning, nothing goes better with coffee than *more* coffee," Nancy joked, handing Terry her empty mug. "Can you get me a free refill while you're up?"

"Anything for a caffeine-starved freshman," Terry said. "Wouldn't want you to fail on account of me. Cream? Sugar?"

"Milk," Nancy said. "Just a little."

He set his mug on the table and went over to the counter to fill Nancy's mug.

Nancy had met Terry, a senior, through the Focus Film Society, a campus film club of which Terry was president. Terry had initially been interested in dating Nancy, but she'd made it clear that she was committed to Jake. Since then, Terry had become a good friend. Nancy didn't see him often, but they always had fun when they did get together.

A few weeks ago Jake had seen Nancy with Terry and accused Nancy of cheating on him with Terry—which was something Nancy would never do. The fact that Jake could assume she was cheating had made Nancy wonder how well Jake knew her. Fortunately, they'd gotten past that. Even though Jake wasn't crazy about Terry, he accepted their friendship.

Terry reminded Nancy of Ned Nickerson, her ex-boyfriend from home. The two guys were very similar, both tall and athletic with strong facial features and gorgeous eyes. Both had deep, sexy voices.

"And what makes you think I might fail?" Nancy asked as Terry sat down opposite her. He straddled a chair and dropped his book bag on the floor. "Don't you have more confidence in me than that?"

Terry tore his flaky croissant in two and handed half to Nancy. "I was just joking. If anyone fails, it'll be me. I've got a killer statistics exam in"—he glanced at his Swiss Army watch—"twenty minutes." He groaned.

"Drink up," Nancy recommended. She took a sip of hot coffee and a bite of the croissant. "Thanks for breakfast. I forgot about the food part."

"No problem." Terry smiled at her. "So, you have a test or something?"

"A Western civ quiz," Nancy said. "You have to study just as hard for a quiz as for a test, but you get only a few points if you do well."

"I know," Terry agreed. "I hate quizzes. I think there should just be one final exam. That would be it. One test, one hundred percent of your grade. Three hours, and it'd be all finished."

Nancy laughed. "More like three hours and I'd be finished! That would be awful. We'd all flunk for sure and have major anxiety attacks."

"Well, maybe you'll like this idea better," Terry said, sipping his coffee. "The Tivoli theater downtown is showing Marc Bartique's latest film—you know him, the French director who did *Remember Bombay*. I was wondering if you'd want to check it out with me. Maybe we could bring it to the Film Society next semester. We could do a Marc Bartique weekend. What do you think?"

Nancy hesitated. She did want to see the movie—she loved Marc Bartique's other films—

but she wasn't sure she should see it with Terry. Jake might not appreciate that.

"Look"—Terry put his hand on Nancy's arm—"I'm not asking you *out,* out. I'm just asking if you want to go as, you know, friends. This would not be a date."

"I know," Nancy said, but she was glad to hear Terry say it anyway. That meant he understood she was interested only in being friends—nothing more. "You know what? I'd love to see the movie. I think Jake would, too. I'll bring him along," Nancy said.

Terry nodded. "Sounds good. How about Wednesday night? That'll give us something to look forward to after your quiz and my statistics exam." He glanced at his watch again. "Uh-oh. Got to put in some last-second cramming. See you later."

"Good luck! Thanks for breakfast," Nancy called after him, waving the last bite of croissant in the air. Pastry crumbs dropped onto her study notes. She quickly brushed them off and got back to work. She had a quiz to take—in less than an hour!

George Fayne squinted at the alarm clock beside her bed. "Eight-thirty?" she cried. "It's already eight-thirty?"

George had set her alarm for seven so she could jog before her first class. She must have turned it off and fallen back to sleep. Now she'd be lucky if she even made her first class.

What a way to start the week, George thought with a moan. As if Mondays weren't bad enough. She swung her long legs over the edge of the bed and sat up, rubbing her face and trying to come to life. She felt as if she'd been run over by a truck.

A large truck with heavy tires, she decided as she stood up and looked in the mirror. Her curly dark hair was sticking out every which way; her face was creased from becoming one with her pillow; and her brown eyes were bloodshot.

Time to hit the shower! She leaned down to grab her basket of shampoo and soap from under the bed. When she stood up, the room seemed to be tilted on one side. George lost her balance and fell onto the bed; the other furniture in the room swirling in front of her eyes. Her stomach was churning as she felt herself start to sweat.

Abruptly she knew she was going to throw up.

George dropped her basket and raced down the hall to the bathroom. Now to add to her Monday morning troubles, she was sick.

"You don't faint at the sight of blood, do you?" the doctor asked.

Ginny Yuen looked across the desk at Dr. Hazel Mosely, head of the research department at Weston General Hospital. "No . . . I mean, I never have." The way Dr. Mosely was talking, Ginny was going to be very challenged by her volunteer job in the hospital's research lab.

"Good. Because you're going to be seeing a few things that might make you squeamish," Dr. Mosely continued. "Categorizing blood samples on slides, for example. And you're going to have to be tough, even if you don't feel tough."

Ginny nodded. "Okay. I can do that," she said.

"Occasionally you'll interact directly with patients," Dr. Mosely told Ginny. "I expect you to handle every situation as a professional." Ginny nodded again, smiling slightly. "I was a volunteer in pediatrics," she said. "I'm used to being around patients and their families."

"Yes, I know. You did come highly recommended." Dr. Mosely closed Ginny's file and tapped it against the desk. "Let me go find the resident you've been assigned to. If he's not busy, he'll come to meet you and show you around the department."

"That would be great," Ginny said, smiling.

After Dr. Mosely left the office, Ginny stood up and paced back and forth, examining the doctor's diplomas that were framed and hanging on the wall. Ginny tried to picture having her own name on so many degrees. She had so much work to do before she graduated from Wilder University in four years—never mind going on to medical school.

For a second Ginny wondered what her ex-boyfriend, Ray Johansson, would say if he could see her now. She was dressed in a starched green lab coat, her long black hair pulled back into a neat bun. She looked so conservative, so professional—the exact opposite of the way she'd been with Ray: spontaneous, offbeat, laid-back. With him she had spent her time writing lyrics to rock songs instead of studying chemistry, the way she did now with her good friend Frank Chung.

Ray would probably say that Ginny was giving in to her parents, who had pressured her to stay in the premed program. Maybe she was. She'd hoped that volunteering at the hospital would make her feel more committed to premed.

So far, she wasn't sure. There were plenty of things she'd rather be doing than sitting in Hazel Mosely's office, waiting to meet the resident she'd be assisting.

What if he's incredibly demanding? she thought. What if he thinks I don't know enough to help him with his research?

Ginny was still pacing and worrying when the door opened. Dr. Mosely came back into her office, followed by a drop-dead gorgeous guy, the most gorgeous guy Ginny had ever seen, with broad shoulders, smooth straight brown hair, and deep chocolate brown eyes.

Dr. Mosely should have asked if I faint at the sight of gorgeous men, Ginny thought, not blood.

She could barely take her eyes off the doctor's face, his bright smile and his twinkling brown eyes. Even his eyelashes were perfect—thick and dark and curled up at the tips.

"Hello, Ginny. I'm Dr. Malcolm Hendrix." He held out his hand. "It's a pleasure to meet you. I'm looking forward to working together."

"Oh, m-me, too," Ginny sputtered. He had no idea how much! She shook his hand, admiring his strong grip and long, agile fingers. "Thanks for taking me on, Dr. Hendrix."

"Malcolm," he said warmly. "Call me Malcolm, please. We're colleagues now." He smiled at her, and his whole face lit up.

Ginny thought she might melt. All of a sudden premed didn't seem so bad.

"So, can I give you a tour of the hospital?" Malcolm offered.

"I've done some volunteering here," Ginny told him as they walked out into the hall. "But I don't know too much about the research labs."

"Then I'll be happy to show them to you," Malcolm said. "Since that *is* where you'll be spending all your time for the next few months. I hope that doesn't sound boring." He laughed, glancing at Ginny.

"No," Ginny said with a smile. "Not at all." She wouldn't mind spending a few months with Malcolm—anywhere!

* * *

Bess Marvin held the latest issue of *Major Mode* above her head, turning it to the left, then to the right. How could anyone except the skinniest model wear a shirt like that? She couldn't begin to fit into something so tiny. It looked like the size shirt she would have worn in third grade!

She turned the page to the layout on resort wear. All the photographs had been taken either on a yacht or at a beach, and featured models in bikinis or slinky backless dresses or miniskirts.

Bess was getting ready for a frigid, Midwestern winter. It was time for her to order boots and thermal underwear, not bathing suits.

But maybe that was good. Bess stared at a picture of an especially skinny model in a bikini. She didn't exactly feel like baring herself like that, not right now. How did models keep their thighs as thin as twigs?"

Turn the page, Bess told herself. Read an article about how it's better to have a good personality. "Find Your Zodiac Love Mate" was the next article.

The telephone beside her bed started ringing, and Bess jumped, startled. She'd been lying in bed for hours because she just couldn't find a good reason to make herself get up. She felt like hiding from the world.

Her roommate, Leslie King, had been in class all morning, so Bess had to answer the phone.

But she wasn't sure she wanted to talk to anyone. Finally she decided to take the risk.

"Hello?" she said into the receiver. She pushed her shoulder-length blond hair back from her forehead.

"Hi, Bess. It's Ned. How are you doing?"

Bess grinned. "Ned! Wow, it's great to hear from you." Ned Nickerson was an old friend from back home in River Heights. He and one of Bess's best friends, Nancy Drew, had dated for a long time. They'd all become very close during high school, spending most of their time together, along with Bess's cousin, George Fayne.

Ever since Nancy, Bess, and George had gone off to Wilder—Ned went to Emerson College—their relationships had changed. Nancy and Ned had broken up, while in the last few weeks, Bess and Ned had become better friends.

Bess's boyfriend, Paul Cody, had recently been killed when his motorcycle was hit by a drunk driver. While Bess was at home, recovering from Paul's death and her own injuries, she had come to rely on Ned. He had taken a little time off from school to visit Bess, and they had spent several hours together, both in person and on the phone.

Ned always managed to make Bess feel better. He seemed to understand what she was going through, even though he'd never experienced anything so shattering in his own life.

"It's good to hear your voice," Ned said. "What are you up to? Studying?"

"Hardly," Bess admitted. "Unless you count checking out the latest, hottest clothes and makeup trends as studying."

"Maybe if you were in fashion school?" Ned said with a small laugh. "Okay, so, it's Monday, and you're sitting around your room reading magazines. Is there anything else I need to know? Like, should I picture a can of soda beside you, or—"

"Ned, this is embarrassing, but I haven't even gotten out of *bed* yet this morning," Bess said.

"Bess, it's afternoon," Ned said. "Two o'clock, last time I checked."

Bess groaned. "Oh, no. Is it really? Whoops." She hadn't meant to blow off the whole day.

"Hey, look at it this way, you'll be just in time for dinner if you get up soon," Ned teased.

"Or I'll be ready for bed without having to change my clothes," Bess joked. The truth was, she didn't feel like laughing. There was something a little absurd, and a little sad, about spending an entire Monday in bed.

"Ned, I didn't tell you, but . . . I'm in training," she said. "My sorority's having one of those twenty-four-hour sleepathons next week—"

"Uh-huh. I bet," Ned said. "Well, I hope that at least you missed some heinous class or test or something."

"No such luck. All my papers are due at the end of the week," Bess said. "In fact, I should probably throw these magazines out the window and hit the books."

"Don't do that," Ned said.

"Why not?" Bess asked. "You're the one who's always encouraging me to study and bring out my academic side—"

"All I meant was, don't throw the magazines out the window," Ned said. "You might hit someone, and anyway, you should recycle them."

This time Bess laughed for real.

"Start studying," Ned went on. "Do you think you can get all your papers done by Friday?"

"Probably," Bess said, stretching her left arm over her head. It had fallen asleep from leaning on it for so many hours.

"Good. I was thinking about coming to Wilder for the weekend." Ned said. "And I don't want to spend half my time sitting next to you in the library while you—"

"Wait a second. You're coming *here?* This weekend? That's great!" Bess said, thrilled. "When? What time?"

"Friday after my last class," Ned said. "I can probably stay until Sunday. Does that sound good?"

"No," Bess said.

"It doesn't?" Ned asked. "Well, I could come Saturday, I guess, or . . ."

EAU CLAIRE DISTRICT LIBRARY

"Ned, it's not *good*. It's way better than *good*," Bess said. "This gives me a reason to get out of bed and do my work. I guess I kind of needed that. Thanks."

"No problem," Ned said. "Except . . . how am I supposed to motivate myself to work now?"

"Simple," Bess said. "Think about how much fun you're going to have at Wilder. Because, as everyone knows, the social life here is at least ten times better than it is at Emerson."

"Yeah, yeah. So you keep saying. We'll see," Ned said. "In the meantime, take care of yourself. Don't stay in bed tomorrow, too."

"I won't," Bess promised. "I think I'm coming down with a really bad case of bed head."

"With your long hair that could be a total disaster," Ned teased. "Better take a shower and get to work on it. I know you couldn't bear a bad hair day."

"Thanks a lot!" Bess laughed. "I thought you were calling to cheer me up!"

She hung up the phone and discovered she was smiling. For the first time that day she felt she had a reason to get out of bed.

EAU CLAIRE DISTRICT LIBRARY

CHAPTER 2

So, what did you think? Could you stand spending all your time in a dark room with no windows?"

Ginny gazed up at Malcolm. "It's not *that* dark in the lab."

Malcolm nodded. "Right. Not with all those hideous fluorescent lights shining down on you."

"Right." Ginny smiled. "Anyway, I can always go down to the solarium if I'm feeling sun deprived," she said. "I think the lab's really nice, actually. Talk about state-of-the-art equipment."

"Yeah, for a smaller town, Weston's got an amazing hospital," Malcolm agreed. "Which is the reason I decided to do my residency here."

"Oh, you're probably really busy, so I shouldn't keep you," Ginny said, suddenly feeling guilty for taking up so much of Malcolm's time. "Thanks for showing me all the lab equipment. I'll be totally ready to work when I come in tomorrow."

"Great," Malcolm said. He glanced at the clock on the wall, near the elevator. "Actually, I don't have to be anywhere for the next half hour. How about grabbing a cup of coffee with me?"

"Coffee?" Ginny repeated. She couldn't believe Malcolm wanted to keep hanging out with her. "Um, sure, that sounds nice."

"Well, it would sound even better if it weren't the cafeteria's coffee," Malcolm said. "I hope you have a strong stomach." He guided Ginny toward the elevator, pushed the Down button, and waited, leaning against the wall.

"Dr. Mosely told me I'd have to be extra tough to work here," Ginny said. "But I didn't know she was talking about the cafeteria food!"

Malcolm laughed. "Oh, yeah. It's legendary."

The elevator doors opened with a loud *bing*. A tall man stepped out. "Good afternoon, Dr. Hendrix," he said.

"Hello, Dr. Willard," Malcolm replied. "I'm going down for a cup of coffee. Will I see you in the lab later?"

"If I'm not there, come by my office," Dr. Willard said. He glanced at Ginny, then strode off down the hall.

She followed Malcolm into the elevator, trying

to imagine what it would be like to be called "Dr. Yuen" one day.

"How did the quiz go?" Jake Collins asked, setting down his cheeseburger. He and Nancy were eating dinner in the Cave, a grubby restaurant in the basement of Rand Hall, the architecture building.

"Quiz?" Nancy repeated. She took a sip of her iced tea. "Oh, the Western civ quiz. I've forgotten about it already."

"Selective memory?" Jake teased, brushing at a crumb on his blue denim shirt. "Did you block it out because it was so terrible?"

"No, it was okay." Nancy pushed her hair behind her ears.

"How were your other classes?" Jake asked.

"Pretty good," Nancy said with a shrug.

Jake cast a questioning glance at Nancy as she dipped a piece of chicken into barbecue sauce. She wasn't acting like herself tonight, he thought. It was as if she wasn't all there. After their great weekend together, he thought she'd be more in tune with him.

"So, how are you doing, other than classes?" Jake asked. "You seem a little preoccupied. Is it Bess? Or your dad? Or—"

"No, everything's fine." Nancy glanced at Jake and gave him a wry smile. "I mean, considering it's Monday."

"Right," Jake said nervously. He was staring into Nancy's gorgeous blue eyes, but he felt as if she were a million miles away.

"Hey, I ran into Terry today," Nancy announced all of a sudden. "He mentioned that a new Marc Bartique film is playing downtown. I told him you and I might want to go with him. Is Wednesday okay?"

Jake was about to put a french fry in his mouth. He stopped midair, and a dollop of ketchup dripped onto the table. "What?"

"I said, I told Terry the three of us could go to the Tivoli together on Wednesday and—"

"So I did hear you right the first time," Jake said. "I just couldn't believe it, though." He shook his head.

"Why not?" Nancy asked. "Is Wednesday night bad for you? We can change the day, maybe go on the weekend."

"It's not the day. Nancy, you know I don't like Terry, for starters. Also, he's interested in you," Jake argued. "So why would the *three* of us go anywhere together?"

Nancy looked stunned. "I didn't think it would be a problem. I mean, Terry knows that I'm your girlfriend."

"Does he?" Jake asked, growing hotter by the second. "He sure doesn't act that way—asking you out to the movies—"

"As a *friend*," Nancy insisted. "What do you

think he's going to do—send you to buy popcorn so he can make a pass at me?"

"I wouldn't put it past him," Jake muttered under his breath. "Nancy, you and I can hardly find time to spend together as it is. Now we're going to the movies—with Terry tagging along? Come on, give me a break!"

Nancy stared at Jake, her eyes flashing with anger. "Friends go to movies together. It's no big deal. But you know what? You don't *have* to go to the movie at all. Terry and I can go alone," Nancy said, standing up. She pulled a ten-dollar bill out of her purse and dropped it on the table. "Call me when you're willing to talk like a rational human being." She turned and left.

Jake watched her go, her shiny strawberry blond hair swaying back and forth as she walked briskly away from him. He put his head in his hands. They had just had a great weekend together. Now what had he done?

"Nancy, what do you think?" Kara Verbeck held up a pink- and beige-striped sweater. "Does this go with these brown jeans?"

Nancy glanced up at her roommate. She and Kara shared a bedroom that was in a suite with six other freshman women, including Ginny Yuen, who was sitting on Kara's bed waiting for Kara to go to the library with her. "Sure, that sweater looks good."

"See, I told you," Ginny said.

"Okay, but if I have brown pants on, then I can't wear these shoes, because they'll clash." Kara stared into her closet at the tangle of shoes on the floor. "But if I wear the black ones, they won't look right either. . . ."

"Kara, we're only going to the *library,*" Ginny said, laughing. "No one's going to notice your shoes."

"That's where you're wrong," Kara said. "When you're sitting in a study carrel, all you can see are feet!"

Nancy grinned. "You know, Kara, if you spent half as much time studying at the library as you do checking out shoes—"

"I wouldn't have a C average," Kara said. "Yeah, yeah, I know. But I wouldn't have nearly as much fun either. Okay, help me out, Ginny. What goes with burgundy . . ."

Nancy shook her head and went back to reading the latest issue of *Wilder Times,* the school newspaper she wrote for. Even though she and Kara had been roommates since school began, she still couldn't get over Kara's obsession with clothes. If Kara had her way, she would go shopping every afternoon.

While Kara and Ginny talked about Ginny's latest volunteer assignment at the hospital, Nancy flipped through the paper. She was taking a break before starting her assigned reading for the night.

"Dream Student Vacations" was the article she had just been reading. Funny, she thought, I was just dreaming about taking a vacation!

There was a knock at the door. "Knock, knock. Can I come in?" Jake called out.

Nancy turned over on her bed. Had Jake come to make up already? "Are you decent?" she asked Kara.

"If you consider pants that are too short to go with these clogs decent," Kara replied.

"Come on in!" Nancy called, even though she wasn't sure she was ready to see Jake. She was still angry about what he had said about Terry an hour ago.

"Hi." Jake walked into the room. "Hi, Kara. Hi, Ginny."

"Hey, Jake. What did you bring us?" Ginny pointed to the bag in Jake's hand.

"Fresh, hot from the oven, chocolate-chip cookies," Jake said. He opened up the bag and held it out to Nancy. "Also known as a peace offering."

"Wow. You made these for me?" Nancy asked.

"No, but the guy at Lane's Bakery did," Jake said. "If I tried to make them, I wouldn't have been here until tomorrow morning to apologize. Anyway, I am sorry. I totally and completely overreacted," Jake said. "I don't know what got into me."

"That's okay," Nancy said. "Anyone who

brings me hot cookies can be forgiven." She smiled at Jake.

He sat down on the bed next to her and put an arm around her waist. "I'm sorry I ruined our dinner. I acted like a jerk."

Nancy put her finger on his lips. "That's enough apologizing. Time to kiss and make up." She leaned over and pressed her lips to Jake's mouth.

He held her close, returning the kiss. "Mmm. This almost makes arguing worth it."

Kara cleared her throat. "Hello? *Some* of us are still in the room."

"Yes, you certainly are," Jake said, with a teasing glance at Ginny and Kara. "Though *some* of us have no idea why."

"We should be going, anyway. If we don't hit the Rock soon, we won't get a carrel," Ginny said, referring to Rockhausen Library.

"All right, all right. I guess I'm ready," Kara said with an exaggerated sigh. "Give me a cookie and we're out of here."

"Take the whole bag," Jake said, holding it behind him as he started kissing Nancy again.

Kara grabbed the bag from him, and she and Ginny left the room.

"I thought they'd never leave," Jake said. He hugged Nancy tightly.

Nancy loved the way Jake held her. For a few moments he made her forget everything.

"So. Am I acting rational yet?" Jake asked, running his fingers through Nancy's hair.

"Let's see—apologizing, bringing me presents, kissing me . . ." Nancy tapped him lightly on the nose. "Well, it's a *start,* anyway."

"Good." Jake smiled. "I guess I just feel sensitive about the whole Terry thing. Anyway, I can't go to the movie Wednesday night—I have a history review session that I can't miss."

"Oh." Nancy felt disappointed. "I wish you weren't busy. You and I haven't been to a movie in a long time."

"No kidding," Jake grumbled. "I practically forgot whether you like your popcorn with butter or without."

"Without," Nancy said. "I'll tell you all about the movie afterward. Whether it's better than *Remember Bombay* or—"

"Hold on," Jake said, his forehead creased with concern. "You're still going to the movie?"

"Of course," Nancy said. "Terry and I have to evaluate it for the Film Society."

"So you're going without me—and with Terry," Jake concluded.

"Right," Nancy said. She could tell that Jake was getting angry again. Just the mention of Terry's name seemed to set him off. "Why are you looking at me like that? You're acting as if I'm going on a date with Terry. I'm not," Nancy said. Hadn't they been through this already?

"Yes, you are," Jake replied. "If you go to the movies with a guy, Nancy, it's pretty much a date, whether you *call* it that or not."

"No, it isn't," Nancy said. "Terry and I are just friends. Look, if you can't handle the idea of my being friends with a guy, it means that you don't trust me. And if you can't trust me, then we really don't have a relationship."

As soon as the words were out of Nancy's mouth, she realized she'd been thinking that for a long time. She just hadn't wanted to acknowledge the fact that her feelings for Jake had changed. No matter how much fun they'd had the past weekend, she still didn't feel as close to him as she once had. She thought their weekend together had erased all the negativity between them, but apparently it hadn't changed a thing.

"What are you saying? I trust you," Jake argued.

"No." Nancy shook her head. "You don't." She took a deep breath. "That's one of the reasons I don't think we should see each other anymore."

"One of the reasons? You mean, you've been making a list?" Jake asked.

"No, of course not," Nancy said. "But, Jake, you and I both know that things haven't been going that well between us lately."

"That's because you keep insisting on going out with Terry," Jake said angrily.

"Terry has nothing to do with this!" Nancy cried. "It's about you and me, Jake."

"Terry has *everything* to do with this," Jake insisted.

"No. It's not Terry. It's you and me. Two people who shouldn't be together anymore," Nancy said. "Not if we're going to fight like this every other day."

"Fine. Consider this fight over, then." Jake stormed out of the room, slamming the door behind him.

Nancy sat on her bed, staring at the closed door. Jake was wrong. He knew as well as she did that they had problems that had nothing to do with Terry.

She found her thoughts drifting to Ned. Their relationship had been so ideal. Dating someone new will never be like that, Nancy realized. We knew each other inside and out, the good and the bad. Will anyone ever understand me that well again?

CHAPTER 3

"What can I do this weekend that would be special?" Stephanie Keats asked her roommate, Casey Fontaine. They were hanging out in their room after their Tuesday morning classes. Stephanie had come back to the suite to change her clothes because she couldn't stand to wear the same outfit all day. Not only that, but her makeup needed a major overhaul.

"Gee, I don't know. Donate all your old designer clothes to Goodwill? Volunteer at the humane society? *Study?*" Casey suggested with a teasing grin.

Stephanie sighed loudly. "I'm not talking about doing something special for society. I'm talking about doing something special for—"

"Yourself? What a shock!" Casey said.

Stephanie shook her head. Really, the amount of abuse she took was unreal. Just because she had a healthy amount of self-esteem, everyone wanted to jump all over her. "Not for myself. For Jonathan."

"Oh." Casey looked sort of shocked. "For Jonathan?"

"Yes. Why is that so hard to believe?" Stephanie asked. She and Jonathan Baur had been seeing each other for a while, and only recently they'd reached a new, more serious level in their relationship. That was *after* Stephanie had acted like a real jerk and cheated on Jonathan by seeing other guys. Those days were over. She wasn't going to blow it this time.

Jonathan was a manager at Berrigan's Department Store, where Stephanie had a part-time job. He was tall and handsome and kind, and Stephanie was completely in love with him.

"Well, you guys have had your problems," Casey said slowly.

"Which is exactly why I want to do something special for him," Stephanie declared, fingering her long black hair as she looked at herself in the full-length mirror. "So, do you have any ideas? I thought maybe you'd have another brainstorm." Casey had arranged for Jonathan to meet Stephanie a week ago, when he wouldn't have anything to do with her, by telling him he was going to meet someone for a job interview.

"Well, as a matter of fact, I do have one. If you want to have a really romantic weekend, leave campus. Like, immediately if not sooner. Nancy went away with Jake this past weekend, and they had a great time."

Stephanie looked at Casey, raising one eyebrow. "Oh, yeah. They had such a good time they broke up."

"What? They did?" Casey asked.

"Yes. I was coming home last night and Jake was storming off down the hall—as usual, I might add. I asked him what was wrong, and he practically bit my head off. Really, why can't people keep their problems to themselves," Stephanie mused out loud.

Then she thought about it for a second. Just because it hadn't worked for Nancy and Jake, that didn't mean she and Jonathan couldn't go away for the weekend and do it right. Somehow the thought of sweeping Jonathan off his feet with a weekend trip was very romantic.

She could just hear him now, saying how he couldn't leave the store for the weekend, how he wouldn't be able to take the time off. She'd have to make sure he could go. She'd have to take the matter totally out of his hands.

"But you know what?" she said to Casey. "I think I will take your advice and go away this weekend. I'm going to do things a little differently, though. I'm going to take Jonathan by surprise. He won't know we're going anywhere until I kidnap him."

"Kidnap him?" Casey repeated. "Do you think that's a good idea?"

Stephanie grinned, already making plans in her head. "I think it's a great idea."

Ginny kept one eye on the microscope and one eye on Malcolm, who was working beside her. She hadn't been able to stop looking at him all afternoon. It was beginning to interfere with her work.

I'd like to look at *him* under the microscope, she thought. Ginny had a feeling Malcolm would make a much more interesting study than the blood sample she was studying just then. She'd never had to fight so hard to keep her mind on her work.

Ginny finally gave in and walked over to Malcolm, who was sitting at his desk, going through some files. "What's keeping you so busy?" she asked.

"Filing. Can you believe it?" Malcolm asked, shaking his head. "I went to medical school so I could alphabetize all day? I don't think so."

Ginny smiled. "Come on, you haven't been filing *all* day, have you?"

"No. I'm just looking for a particular file. I'm helping Dr. Willard with a project. Actually, we could probably use your help at some point," Malcolm said.

"Dr. Willard? Is he the man you said hello to yesterday at the elevator?" Ginny asked.

"Yes, that's him. Dr. Thomas Willard's the top cardiologist here," Malcolm said. "He's incredible. Weston's lucky to have him, considering every major hospital in the country's tried to hire him away."

"Wow, he's that good?" Ginny asked. "And you get to work with him? Cool."

"Yeah, it is pretty cool," Malcolm admitted with a smile. "You'll get to work with him, too, if you stick around."

"Of course I'll stick around," Ginny told him. "So what kind of project is it?" she asked. "I mean, if it's okay for you to tell me. You don't have to."

"No, it's all right," Malcolm said. "The whole research department knows about it, and you're a member of the research team now."

Ginny loved the way Malcolm included her in things. He treated her as a peer, not a student.

"Dr. Willard's been testing a new kind of heart medication. It's totally different from anything that's available right now. It's designed specifically for people who've already had one heart attack. It prevents a second one. The medication is called Alpha Two."

"Sounds like a space shuttle," Ginny joked.

"It does, doesn't it? Anyway, if all goes well, we should get the drug approved by the FDA in a couple of months. And then Dr. Willard's going to be in even *more* demand."

"And if you're working on the project, too, won't it help your career?" Ginny asked.

"I hope so. I don't know how much more of this filing I can take!" Malcolm said. He sifted through the files a few more times. "Aha! Here it is. Patient 117848."

"So you're using this drug on patients already?" Ginny asked. "I thought you'd test it on animals or—"

Malcolm shook his head. "Not at this stage. Personally I don't like animal testing, but in the first phases of trying out a medication, it can be informative. Anyway, at this point, we've got records from hundreds of patients who volunteered to try the medication. We're tracking their progress closely. So far, it's helped nearly all of them."

"That's fantastic," Ginny said.

"You know what? I think *you're* fantastic," Malcolm said. "We've never had a student volunteer with as much positive energy."

"Really?" Ginny asked. "Do you think I might have—you know, what it takes to be a doctor someday?"

"Definitely," Malcolm said, nodding. "Do you want to meet some of the patients in our study?"

"I'd love to," Ginny said.

"Great. Several of them are coming in tomorrow for their monthly blood tests. Maybe you could plan to be here," Malcolm said.

"That sounds great," Ginny said, hardly believing what she was saying. Watching a bunch of blood tests—great? Since when?

Since Malcolm was going to be there with her, that's when, she thought, glancing at him again. There was something irresistible about his smile. And so far, Ginny didn't feel like resisting.

"Well, better get back to work," Malcolm said.

"Right. Work," Ginny said awkwardly. At the moment work was the last thing on her mind.

"Want to sit here?" Bess pointed to a round table at the Cave.

"Sure. Looks good," Nancy said.

"Whatever." George dropped her tray onto the table, sounding exhausted.

Nancy slid into a seat. That's funny, she thought. The last time I was here, Jake and I sat at the same table.

Somehow it didn't make her sad. It was almost as if, right then, she had no feelings at all about Jake. It was as if the fact that she and Jake were no longer together hadn't hit her yet.

Now it was time to break the news to Bess and George. Nancy had a feeling that would make it seem real. "I have something kind of big to tell you guys," she began. "It's, uh, over between me and Jake."

"*Over* over? Or maybe-you'll-get-back-together-in-a-couple-of-days over?" Bess asked, leaning forward in her chair. "Because I thought you guys kind of broke up before."

"This time it's really over. As in, completely. We had an argument last night," Nancy admitted. "It was kind of stupid, really. I wanted to go see a movie with Terry. Actually I wanted both of us to go. But Jake couldn't go so he didn't want me to go, either. It was your basic I-don't-trust-you-with-another-guy scenario."

"So what did you say?" George asked.

"I told him that if he couldn't trust me, we didn't have much of a relationship," Nancy said. "You know, we've been fighting about the same stuff over and over lately. We just couldn't figure out a way to make it work for both of us."

"So, how do you feel?" Bess asked. "Were you upset? Did you cry?"

"Would I be a horrible person if I told you I don't feel that bad?" Nancy asked.

"No," George said. "I mean, not every relationship has to end with some huge scene."

"But I was in love with him once," Nancy said. "Or at least I thought I was." She wasn't sure anymore. Had her feelings for Jake ever gone as deep as the ones she'd had for Ned? She'd felt more serious about Ned, more committed to their staying together and working out every problem. Until she'd come to Wilder, that is.

"I'm sure I'll miss Jake," Nancy said. "Eventually. But right now, I'm still too mad at him." She took a bite of her pasta and glanced at the full plate of Caesar salad in front of George. Since George was so athletic, she usually had a huge appetite. But she hadn't eaten a thing.

"What's the matter, George? Aren't you hungry?" Nancy asked.

"No . . . yes . . . I don't know. I feel hungry," George said. "But then I try to put a piece of lettuce in my mouth, and the thought of eating makes me feel sick all over."

"You do look a little pale, still. Maybe it wasn't a twenty-four-hour bug you had," Bess suggested. "Maybe it was like a twenty-eight-and-a-half-hour bug."

"And how many seconds?" George smiled wanly. "Whatever it is, I hope it'll leave me alone soon. I feel horrible."

Nancy would never tell her, but she didn't think George looked so hot, either. "Maybe you should go back to your room and lie down for a while," she suggested.

"I'd love to," George said, "but I can't. I missed all my classes yesterday, and . . ."

"You've been dying to hear a lecture ever since?" Bess asked. "Please, I'd die for an excuse to miss classes today. Only I skipped them all yesterday, so I have to go."

"You skipped all of them?" Nancy asked, surprised. "Did you have the stomach bug, too?"

"No. More like the *bed* bug," Bess said. "I just didn't feel like getting out of it."

"But you're okay?" Nancy asked. She didn't want to push Bess. She knew Bess got irritated by everyone's constantly asking her how she felt. But Nancy really wanted to know if her friend was doing okay.

"Yeah. Actually, after I talked to Ned, I felt a lot better," Bess said, popping a potato chip into her mouth.

"You talked to Ned?" Nancy asked, trying not to sound surprised.

"Sure. He called me yesterday, just when I was about to take a quiz on my ideal mate in the zodiac," Bess said.

"Huh?" George looked confused. "Is that a new class you're taking?"

"No. I was reading *Major Mode*. Like, issues from the past six months," Bess explained. "One after the other, after the other, after—"

"So how's Ned?" Nancy asked. She felt kind of awkward, having to ask Bess for information about Ned. Weren't she and Ned supposed to be the closest?

"He's good," Bess said. She sipped her diet soda. "You know, he's been such a good friend to me ever since Paul died. He always knows what to say."

Nancy nodded. "He does, doesn't he?" She couldn't count the number of times Ned had consoled her and made things easier for her.

"Wait, I didn't tell you guys the best part yet—about Ned's calling, I mean," Bess said, sitting up straighter. "He's coming to visit this weekend!"

"He's coming to Wilder? Really?" George asked, sounding surprised.

She couldn't be half as shocked as Nancy was. Ned was visiting Wilder in a few days? And he hadn't told her—he'd told Bess instead? That was weird.

Nancy wondered if Ned had somehow found out about her breakup with Jake. But that was impossible—who would he have heard it from? Bess had only found out a few minutes ago.

But his coming to visit Wilder for the first time since they'd broken up—right when Nancy and Jake had split—didn't seem like a coincidence. Maybe we're both thinking about each other right now. Maybe Ned wants us to get back together, Nancy thought. And as much as she'd thought she was over Ned, the flutter of excitement she felt told her that she still had feelings for him, feelings she'd never had for Jake, or anyone else.

"Maybe we can all go out together Friday night, when he gets here," Bess said. "To Club

Z or the Underground. I told him Wilder has a better social life than Emerson has—now it's up to us to prove it to him."

Nancy smiled. It was great to hear Bess so excited about something. "Hey, I'm up for it if you are," she said enthusiastically.

"I'll try to recover by then," George said, rubbing her stomach. "But I'm not making any promises."

"Maybe you should go to the campus health center," Bess said. "You've gone from pale to green in the last two minutes."

"Maybe I will," George said, pushing her plate away from her. "Or maybe I'll just skip lunch today and hope for the best."

Bess stared at the framed art print on the wall of her counselor's office. It had brightly colored swirls. Bess was always worried her counselor might ask her what she saw in the painting, as if it were a Rorschach test. The print reminded her of something she might have painted in kindergarten.

"So, how's the week been?" Victoria Linden asked, crossing her legs after she sat down in a large brown leather chair facing Bess.

"I don't feel so sad anymore. It's more like . . . I'm just not in the same frame of mind as everyone else. I mean, all anyone talks about is who's dating whom and what party will be the biggest on Friday night."

"You like to socialize, though, don't you?" Victoria asked. "You've mentioned that before. You're in a sorority, and you have a lot of friends."

"Sure, I love to socialize," Bess said. "I mean, I *did.*" She laughed. "Actually, I just had lunch with Nancy and George. I told them Ned's coming to visit this weekend, and we have to go out. So I guess I'm not feeling that bad. I just have to be with the right people, I guess."

"The right people?" Victoria prompted.

"Sure. My best friends from home," Bess said. "It's funny. I've probably been friends with George and Nancy the longest, but lately I feel more connected to Ned. It's like I can totally be myself around him."

"Yourself? You mean, you can relax?" Victoria asked.

Bess nodded. "He doesn't expect me to be one way, or another—and he knows I'm not this fragile piece of china, either. He still teases me and makes fun of me, the way he always has . . . but I can cry on his shoulder, too. I don't have to worry about what he thinks of me."

"What about Nancy and George? Do you worry about what they think of you?" Victoria asked.

"Not really. But . . ." Bess hesitated. How

could she put it, exactly? "It's like they sort of expect me to be the old happy-go-lucky Bess or the Bess whose boyfriend just got killed. And I'm not ever going to be just *one* of those two people. Whatever Paul's death means . . . it's changed me already," Bess said. "Nancy and George don't really see that yet. But Ned does."

Victoria nodded. "That makes sense. Maybe he doesn't have so many expectations for you. But be careful, Bess. You're very vulnerable right now. I'd hate to see you becoming too dependent on Ned or anyone."

"Oh, I don't feel dependent," Bess said. She remembered how she'd felt before Ned called— and after. "I just look forward to seeing him, that's all."

"And you should," Victoria agreed. "That's healthy. In fact, it's a very good sign."

Bess couldn't help feeling that Victoria was holding something back. "But?" she prompted. "Is there a *but* in there somewhere?"

"Just be careful, that's all. You might find yourself feeling more for Ned than you have in the past. He's your friend now, but you might find yourself being attracted to him or sharing lots of personal thoughts with him because he's there for you. Don't forget that he's your friend, not your boyfriend."

"As if I ever would!" Bess laughed. "I can't imagine ever thinking of Ned as more than a

friend. Nancy went out with him for, like, for-
ever!" She shook her head and laughed again.
Imagining herself and Ned on a date had to be
the funniest thing she'd thought of in weeks.

"Bess dropped off a bunch of magazines earlier, when I wasn't feeling well. Help yourself."
George tried to toss the pile of fashion magazines
toward her roommate, Pam Miller, but they slid
onto the floor.

"Man! This is worse than a doctor's office!
Does she have a subscription to everything published in the entire country?" Pam joked, sorting
through the pile.

"Plus some from France," George told her.
"You know when those kids from school come
to the door, selling subscriptions to raise money
for band and stuff like that?" Pam nodded. "Bess
feels so sorry for them, she signs up for one of
each, including *Trout Fishing Monthly* and the
Race Car Rebuilding Manual."

Pam laughed. "You're sure you guys are
cousins?"

"Why?" George said.

"Well, you never read anything but *Sports Il-
lustrated,*" Pam said, pointing to the magazine in
George's hands. "Anyway, how are you feeling?"

"Lousy still," George said. "One more day of
this and I'm going to the campus health center.
I don't care what they do to me." She went back

to reading an article about an up-and-coming track and field star.

Pam suddenly groaned loudly. "Oh, gross."

"What?" George asked.

"This article . . . are you planning to have kids someday?" Pam asked.

"I don't know. Why?" George replied.

"Well, you might want to think twice after you hear this. It's called, 'What Your Mother Didn't Tell You About Being Pregnant.' And there's a list of symptoms that's enough to make you sick, just reading it," Pam said.

"Like what?" George asked.

"First, there's the stuff you probably know already." Pam said. "Nausea, morning sickness, dizziness. That's in the first three months. Then later there's swollen ankles, fatigue, intense mood swings, spider veins, stretch marks, something horrendous called cellulite of the knees, and—"

George sat up straight on her bed. Nausea, morning sickness, dizziness . . . that was what she'd been feeling for the last two days. "Pam?" she said softly. "What day is today?"

"Tuesday," Pam said. "Why?"

"No—I mean, the date," George said, her heart pounding in her chest. Could it be? But how?

"The seventeenth," Pam said.

The magazine dropped from George's hand onto the floor. Her period always came at exactly twenty-eight days. That meant . . . she did a quick calculation in her head. Her period was already five days late!

She was nauseated, she'd had a couple of dizzy spells—this was no stomach flu. She was pregnant!

"George, you okay? How come the date's so important all of a sudden?" Pam asked.

"Oh, I, uh, just remembered I have a paper due tomorrow," George said. She went to her desk and picked up a few books, pretending to look through them. She didn't want to tell Pam her suspicions—not yet. She could hardly believe them herself.

Me—pregnant? George stared at the pages of a book, her eyes filling with tears. What on earth was she going to do?

CHAPTER 4

"Oh, no—are you all done?" Ginny asked, standing in the doorway to the lab.

"Finished," Malcolm said. "Right, Erica?" He turned to the nurse who had just delivered a large tray of test tubes containing blood samples.

"Yes. This should do it for the monthly roundup," Erica said.

"Thanks," Malcolm said. "I appreciate it."

"You're welcome." Erica smiled at Ginny on her way out of the lab. "Sorry you missed all the fun."

Ginny shook her head. "I couldn't get out of my afternoon chem lab. I wanted to, but—"

"School's more important. Don't think you missed anything," Erica told her.

"Erica's right." Malcolm started sorting through the test tubes, examining the labels.

Ginny walked up beside him. "I didn't miss anything?"

"Not really. I mean, you missed meeting a grumpy guy—here he is, number 117848—who scowls at you and complains every time. But he's getting paid plenty for his troubles, testing the placebo," Malcolm said.

"Well, what can I do to help now?" Ginny asked. "How about if I start classifying the blood tests and preparing the slides?"

"No, I'll do that," Malcolm said.

"But that's just grunt work—I can do it," Ginny offered.

"With research this important, there's no such thing as grunt work," Malcolm said.

"Oh. Well, okay," Ginny said. She got the feeling Malcolm didn't trust her with anything important. "Is there anything else I can do?"

"You could make sure all those files are in order—the ones I was going through yesterday," Malcolm said. "Dull but necessary. They seemed totally out of whack last time I checked."

"Okay. Sure." Ginny sat down at the desk with a sigh.

"I know it's a pain, but it has to be done. In the meantime, I'll get these all sorted, then we can easily match all the results when they come in," Malcolm said. He looked over at Ginny. "Hey, Ginny, can I ask you something?"

"Sure."

"Why don't we get together some time, after work? I can tell you all about med school, internships, residency—"

"That is, if you ever get more than three hours off at a time," Ginny said. "Don't residents have to work like thirty-six hours in a row?"

"Nah," Malcolm said. "More like forty-eight."

Ginny laughed. "Uh-huh. I thought so."

"But, it just so happens that I'm free tomorrow night," Malcolm said. "How about dinner?" He reached over and put his hand over Ginny's.

Ginny felt a tingle run up her spine. "Dinner would be nice," she said.

"Great. How about Les Peches?" Malcolm suggested, his brown eyes sparkling as he looked up at her.

"Sounds perfect," Ginny said. Going out to the fanciest restaurant in town with the best-looking young doctor in the whole hospital? She could hardly wait.

Will Blackfeather climbed the stairs of Jamison Hall two at a time, a large bouquet of red and pink carnations cradled in his right arm. He hoped George was in her room. He felt as if he hadn't seen her at all lately.

Whenever they were together, they were surrounded by other people. That was fine most of the time, but what Will wanted tonight was to be alone with his girlfriend—quality time, involving lots of physical contact and absolutely no studying.

Will reached George's floor and walked down the hall to her room. He knocked twice and held the flowers behind his back.

George opened the door. She was wearing a pair of shorts and a sleeveless purple T-shirt. When she turned to let him in, he saw the words "Get Wild at Wilder" printed on the back.

"Hi!" Will greeted her. "Feeling wild tonight?" He leaned over to kiss her.

George turned her head, offering her cheek. "Not very," she said blandly.

Will's lips brushed her cheek. "Are you okay?" he asked. "You sound sort of down."

"Well, I—I just don't feel well," George said.

Will stood back, examining her. George's face was pale, and her eyes lacked their usual sparkle—especially when she saw him. If anything, she looked as if she wished he were gone. "That's too bad," Will said. He brought the flowers out from behind his back. "I was hoping we could go out tonight—have a nice private dinner, maybe go to a movie or hang out at Java Joe's."

George shook her head. "I'm sorry, Will. You know I'd love to. Normally. I mean, usually, that would be great. And these flowers are so beautiful. . . ." Her voice drifted off as she held the flowers closer, inhaling their scent.

"But you're not feeling well? Still?" Will asked.

"Not really." George made a face. "I just don't think I should go out tonight. I don't think I'd be very good company. I can't really eat anything, and I'm tired, too."

"Oh," Will said. "Okay. Well, if you can't, you can't. But maybe I could make you feel better. I could go get you some juice, or something to read—"

"That's okay. Bess brought over a ton of magazines for me," George said.

Will nodded. Why did he suddenly feel so useless?

George grimaced, rubbing her stomach. "Look, I think I'd better go lie down. Sorry to bail on you, but I'm going back to bed."

"Maybe you'll sleep it off," Will said.

"Yeah," George said. "Maybe." She didn't sound convinced. "Thanks for the flowers."

"Oh . . . sure," Will said. He stared at George's sad, sickly expression. He'd never seen her so down before. She was usually so full of energy. "Feel better, okay?"

"I'll try," George managed a faint smile.

"In the meantime, I'll plan something really special—maybe for tomorrow night," Will told her. "You can look forward to it while you recover."

George nodded and started to slowly close the door. "Good night, Will. Thanks for coming over," she said.

"Good night," Will replied. The door closed abruptly, and he found himself standing in the empty hallway. It was the first time in a long time that he could remember not kissing George good night. She was usually so playful and affectionate. Tonight it seemed as though talking to him took all the effort in the world.

She's sick, he reminded himself. It has nothing to do with you.

But Will couldn't help feeling hurt and disappointed as he trudged back downstairs. It was almost as if he was the one person George *didn't* want to see just then.

"Okay, so you've got the idea. More sports, shorter articles," Gail Gardeski said, pacing around the conference room. "That way, every team gets some coverage at some point during the semester."

Nancy glanced across the table at Jake. He glared back at her. He'd been doing that for the entire *Wilder Times* staff meeting.

Obviously, she and Jake weren't going to become friends any time soon—not if he hated her, the way he seemed to.

Nancy tried to picture how much worse things could get if either one of them started dating someone else. How would she feel if she saw Jake with another woman?

"Nancy!"

Nancy blinked and turned toward the head of the table, where Gail was sitting. "Yes?"

"I've only called your name three times," Gail said. "Where were you?"

"Oh—just thinking," Nancy said.

"Well, that's great, but please start *thinking* about writing your next feature story," Gail said brusquely. "I've got an idea I'd like you to pursue—with Jake, actually."

Nancy and Jake glanced at each other. "Uh . . . yeah?" Nancy asked.

"I was in the travel section of the bookstore—I'm thinking about going to Europe next summer," Gail explained. "I saw this book called *The Most Romantic Places in France,* and another one titled *The Best Places to Kiss in Russia—*"

"Indoors, I hope?" Gary Friedman, the newspaper's photographer, said with a laugh. "Or is there a companion book, *How to Deal with Frostbite?*" He munched on a chocolate-covered doughnut.

Gail cleared her throat. "As I was saying, I looked at these guidebooks, and I thought, what a perfect idea for a story!" She looked at Nancy, with a wicked grin. "I mean, if anyone knows the best places to kiss on campus, it's got to be the two staff writers who are in love, right?"

Jake glared at Nancy again.

"Wahoo!" Gary shouted, amid the whistles and catcalls from other staff members.

Nancy smiled uneasily. "Actually—"

"Actually, that's a really *dumb* idea for a story, Gail," Jake declared.

"Really? I thought it was pretty good," Gail said. "What don't you like about it?"

"Everything," Jake said. "Come on, this isn't a high school paper."

"Jake, I don't think it's such a rotten idea," Gary said. "I mean, think about it. You and Nancy would have to do a lot of research—"

"It's juvenile. And I'm not doing it." Jake stood up and walked out of the room.

Gail turned to Nancy. "Well. I know it's not Pulitzer Prize–winning material, but I didn't think it was that bad."

"He's sure in a lousy mood," Gary commented. "What's up with that?"

"I, uh, I'm not sure," Nancy said uneasily. She wasn't about to get into her personal problems in front of everyone. "Maybe he woke up on—"

"The wrong side of campus?" someone suggested.

"The wrong side of reality," someone else added with a laugh.

"Well, if Jake's going to be such a jerk about

it, I could always work on the story with you," Gary said, winking at Nancy. "You know, because it's not really a job one should do all alone—"

"Gary, that's not what I had in mind, okay?" Gail said with a nervous laugh. "I guess you'll have to convince him to help you, Nancy. Jake, that is—not Gary."

Not very likely, Nancy thought. "Yeah. I mean—sure, of course," Nancy said. She thought of all the places she and Jake used to like to go together. The grassy knoll outside the student center, the Lawn, Java Joe's, in a far-off corner in the library stacks . . .

They would probably never kiss there—or anywhere—again. Somehow Nancy hadn't quite realized what breaking up with Jake would mean.

She felt a tear form in the corner of her eye and turned to listen to Gail again, biting her lip to keep from crying. I knew I'd feel bad about this at some point, but did it have to happen in the middle of a staff meeting?

"Nancy? Do you have a second?" Gail asked.

Nancy paused, halfway out of her chair when the meeting ended half an hour later. "Sure." She sat back down and turned to Gail. "What's up?"

"That's what I was going to ask *you,*" Gail said. "What was that all about?"

"What . . ."

"As soon as I mentioned my idea for that article, you turned purple and Jake left the room," Gail said. "Is there a problem between you guys?"

"To tell you the truth, Gail"—Nancy toyed with her pencil, pushing it back and forth across her notebook—"there isn't anything between us. We broke up the other night."

"Oh," Gail said. "Wow. I feel like a jerk. There I was, assigning you a kissing story. I'm sorry."

Nancy shrugged. "It's not your fault. You didn't know."

"How are you doing?" Gail asked.

"Okay, I guess. It was something that kind of had to happen."

"Irreconcilable differences?" Gail said with a faint smile.

"Something like that," Nancy said.

"I can assign the kissing story to someone else," Gail said. "But if you and Jake continue to work on the newspaper—and I'm assuming you will—you're going to have to figure out how to work together. I can't have you guys walking out on meetings just because you're uncomfortable."

Nancy nodded. "I know."

"And when I find Jake later today, I'll tell him the same thing," Gail said. "We all need to cooperate if we want to produce a newspaper. I'm sorry about your breakup, of course. But we can't hold up the newspaper because of it. So, do you think you two can learn to be civil to each other?"

"Honestly, Gail? I don't know right now," Nancy said. "It's too soon. But I promise I won't let our breakup interfere with my work here."

"Good." Gail nodded. "Since you won't be doing the story I suggested, you'll have to come up with another idea—and soon, okay? Well, good luck—with the article and with Jake."

"Thanks." Nancy collected her notebook and pencil and stuffed them into her backpack. She had a feeling that getting along with Jake around the office was going to be a lot harder than thinking of an idea for an article.

Late Wednesday morning, Stephanie stood outside the store manager's office. She hardly dared ask for time off—for herself or for Jonathan, who managed the floor she worked on. She hadn't exactly been a model employee so far.

I'll have to make it sound really good, she thought. Something no one could dare say no to. She couldn't say that she was trying to salvage her love life by kidnapping her boyfriend. Even though it felt like an emergency to *her,* she had a feeling Dave wouldn't have the same opinion.

She knocked on the door, which was ajar, then

poked her head in. "Dave? Do you have a minute?"

"Sure, Stephanie. What can I do for you?" He glanced at the clock above his desk. "Aren't you supposed to be on the floor now?"

Stephanie worked at the cosmetics counter and occasionally helped out in women's accessories. "My shift starts in five minutes," she said.

"Oh. Well, okay," Dave said. "Have a seat. How can I help you?"

Stephanie sat down on the opposite side of his desk. "I have a problem. It involves Jonathan."

"What is it?" Dave's forehead creased. "Isn't he treating you fairly? Is it your schedule—"

"Oh, no!" Stephanie laughed. "My problem isn't with Jonathan. But I need to ask you if he could, uh, have the weekend off. Actually I need to have it off, too."

Dave gave her a disapproving look. "Stephanie, it's already Wednesday. The schedule's made. And you know that in retail we all have to work on weekends."

Stephanie took a deep breath. Then she let out a pathetic-sounding sigh, trying to sound as sad as she could. "I was afraid you'd say that. But, Dave, this isn't just any weekend."

"It isn't?" Dave said, glancing at the calendar.

"No. It's—" She sniffled. "Well, it's my grandmother."

54

"Your grandmother?" Dave repeated, sounding concerned.

"She's not well," Stephanie said. Both her grandmothers were fine. One lived in Florida and spent her days walking on the beach; the other lived in Manhattan, in a penthouse apartment. But Dave didn't need to know that. Stephanie tried to bring tears to her eyes. "I've been trying to find some time to visit her in the hospital. But it's impossible, because either I'm working or in school. There's just no time—"

"Stephanie, it's okay," Dave told her.

"And what if something happens to her," Stephanie went on, sniffling, "and I'm not there, and I never get the chance to—"

"Stephanie, it's all right. You can have the weekend off," Dave interrupted. He pulled a tissue out of the box on his desk and handed it to Stephanie. "Please stop crying."

"I'm sorry. I didn't mean to fall apart like this." She blew her nose. Wow. She never knew she was such a talented actress. "It's just such a stressful situation. That's why I need Jonathan to drive me there. I could never do it on my own."

"No. I can see that," Dave said. He started flipping through the store schedule for that week. "So, what exactly is wrong with your grandmother, if you don't mind my asking?"

Well, she's a little demanding sometimes. And

she hasn't sent me a check in a while. That's about it. "It's her . . . her heart," she told Dave.

"That's unfortunate," Dave said. He tapped a pencil against the schedule. "I guess if I did a little rearranging I could give both of you Saturday off. Jonathan might need to be back Sunday afternoon, though. Could you do that? How far do you need to travel?"

"Oh, not—not far," Stephanie said. "We could definitely get back by Sunday afternoon." She paused. "I have one more favor to ask you, Dave. You know what a workhorse Jonathan is. He can't stand taking time off. And if he finds out I asked you about his schedule, he'll be furious with me." She looked at her lap and dabbed at her eyes with a tissue. "Would you mind not saying anything to him about having Saturday off? I want to be the one who tells him. If he finds out too far ahead of time, he'll probably try to make me drive there by myself, and I—I don't know if I can do that," Stephanie said, starting to cry again.

"No problem," Dave said. "Just make sure he's back on Sunday."

"I will. Thank you for being so understanding," Stephanie said, standing to leave. Not to mention gullible!

Now all she had to do was pick the perfect place for a romantic weekend.

*   *   *

George pulled the belt of her beige trench coat tight and adjusted the large, floppy hat on her head. She was wearing dark sunglasses, and she had wrapped a scarf around her neck.

I probably look like a criminal, she thought. Or a detective. A really bad, obvious detective.

But she had to disguise herself. She didn't want anyone to see her buying a pregnancy test at the drugstore.

George smiled wryly as she pushed open the door and walked into Campus Corner Pharmacy. As concerned as she was, she had to laugh, or she'd go crazy.

She lowered the sunglasses on her nose for a second so she could see where she was going. Then she wound her way to the right aisle, trying not to attract any attention. So far, so good, she thought, standing in front of a wide array of pregnancy tests. Which one should I choose? she wondered. There were so many!

She slipped off the sunglasses to get a better look at all of the boxes as she wandered down the aisle, trying to act casual.

"George? Is that you?"

George felt panic shoot through her. "Uh, Andy!" she said, trying not to sound as nervous as she felt. It was Andy Rodriguez, Will's roommate. What was he doing there? Spying on her?

"What's with the outfit?" Andy asked. "Is it supposed to rain or something?"

George laughed uneasily. "Rain. Ha-ha. No, it's . . . uh . . ." She glanced at the shelf on her right and grabbed a gallon-size bottle of liquid laundry detergent. "It's Wednesday. Which means it's laundry day," she said.

"Laundry day?" Andy repeated.

"Yeah. And I'm out of, like, everything," George said, rolling her eyes. "Jeans, shirts, socks. I put all my clothes in the washer, you know? And then I realized I didn't have any detergent. So I had to run over here."

"What about those machines in the basement, by the washers and dryers that sell little packets of detergent?" Andy said.

"They were sold out," George said. "Completely." Why did she feel as if Andy was giving her the third degree? So she was doing her laundry—so what? Since when was that an issue—or even interesting? "So, what are *you* doing here?" she asked, changing the subject.

Andy held up an Ace bandage. "Gotta wrap my ankle before I meet Will. Basketball at noon, remember?"

George nodded. "Right." Andy and Will played basketball on Mondays, Wednesdays, and Fridays at noon, with a bunch of other guys. But the thought of Will was too much for George just then. She couldn't imagine how he'd feel if he thought she was pregnant. She couldn't imagine telling him.

Not that he'd react badly. In fact, probably the opposite. But somehow, for right now, it was something she wanted to handle on her own. Of course, she didn't even know if it was true yet.

Not that she was going to find out any time soon, with Andy hanging around. She took the bottle of laundry detergent up to the register. "Well, have fun playing basketball," she told Andy as they both paid for their things. George didn't even need detergent, she thought as she handed over six dollars—and she definitely didn't need a gallon of it!

"Have fun doing your laundry," Andy said with a laugh. "Hey, maybe Will and I could bring some of our stuff over, you know, since you're already doing yours—"

"Andy?" George said. "Don't even think about it."

She lifted the giant detergent bottle over her shoulder and walked out of the drugstore. So much for taking the test that morning. She'd have to wait until after her afternoon classes and find another drugstore—on the far side of town.

CHAPTER 5

"Hey, Will, guess who I just ran into?" Andy said as he walked onto the basketball court in the Wilder gym that day at noon.

Will tossed the ball to him. "Who? Michael Jordan? Wait, don't tell me—he wants to join our noon game."

"No. Not Michael—George." Andy laughed, shaking his head. "Man, you should have seen what she was wearing. That girl needs some new clothes."

Will grinned. "Sweats, again?"

"No. Worse," Andy said. He took a shot at the basket. "She had on this raincoat and a giant hat. She looked like my grandmother, almost."

Will rebounded the ball and tossed it to Andy, so he could take another shot. "What do you mean? Is she still sick?"

"Sick? No, she didn't say anything about that."
Andy shrugged. "She looked fine to me. She said
she was doing her laundry. She ran out of clothes,
so that's why she was dressed like that."

But George just did her laundry, Will remembered, on Sunday night. She never made plans on
Sunday nights, because that was when she always
washed her clothes. George was very organized
about stuff like that.

So what was she up to? And if she was feeling
better, then why hadn't she called Will?

"Where did you see her?" Will asked, puzzled.

"That pharmacy, on the west side of campus,"
Andy said. "She had these sunglasses on, like she
didn't want anyone to recognize her. And I can
understand why, with that outfit on."

"So, she was doing her laundry now?" Will
asked. That was odd. He knew she had a lot of
homework to catch up on, after being sick for
two days.

Andy shrugged. "Yeah. I asked her if we could
bring over our clothes. She practically bit my
head off."

"Yeah, well, can you blame her?" Will asked.

"Nah. I was just teasing her," Andy said.

"I wonder why she didn't call me." Will shook
his head.

"You were in class all morning, weren't you?"
Andy said. "Did you want her to page you?
You'll see her tonight, anyway."

"Yeah. You're right," Will said. "It's just that I haven't seen her for a few days because she's been feeling so lousy."

"Well, if she's doing her laundry, it's probably so she has something to wear when you go out later," Andy said. "Unless you like that old-lady trench coat look?"

Will grinned. Andy was right. The fact that George was out and about meant she must be feeling better. And that meant they could go out tonight. He'd call her as soon as he got back to his room. He couldn't wait to have her in his arms again.

Jake was sitting at his desk in the *Wilder Times* office, staring at the bulletin board. "Dinner with Nancy," he'd written on the calendar for that Friday. He picked up a pen and scratched it off. Dinner alone was more like it. Or no dinner, considering the food he had in his apartment right now.

He glanced at the three ideas he'd come up with for his next article: "Write about: pep rally, pesticides on grass, why classes start at ten minutes past the hour." Pretty lame, Jake had to admit. But he wasn't exactly feeling inspired these days.

He heard the outer door to the newspaper office close and crouched over his desk, pretending to work. No doubt it was Gail, coming down to give him another lecture about walking out of staff meetings.

"Hey."

Jake looked up, startled by Nancy's voice. "Oh. I mean, hi," he said.

"I didn't mean to sneak up on you," Nancy said.

"You didn't," Jake replied, trying to keep his cool.

"Well, if you're in the middle of something . . ."

"I was just working up three new story ideas," Jake said. She didn't need to know they were all pathetically lousy.

"I wanted to tell you something. Look, Jake, I'm sorry," Nancy said.

"Sorry?" Jake repeated. He couldn't believe his ears. Was Nancy actually going to apologize for dumping him so she could go to the movies with Terry?

"About the meeting," Nancy said. "About the story Gail mentioned, and—"

"Why are you sorry?" Jake demanded, irritated. "It was Gail's dumb idea, not yours." Jake glanced at Nancy. He couldn't take being close to her like this—not yet. "Anyway, I have to go. I'm late." He stood up, grabbing his denim jacket from the back of the chair.

He rushed out of the office before Nancy could say another word. Whatever she was sorry about, she certainly wasn't sorry she'd broken up with him. That much was clear!

George took a box off the shelf and studied the package. She'd practically run to the drugstore after her last class. She picked up another box and read the directions. She grabbed yet another one. How was she supposed to know which one to pick?

Price, she thought, checking her trench coat pocket for the change left over from buying the laundry detergent earlier that day. She'd have to buy the cheapest one. Generic would be fine.

She put the remaining boxes back and walked up to the front counter, gingerly placing it in front of the clerk.

"All set?" the female salesclerk asked, smiling at George.

She nodded nervously, feeling her face turn pink. "Yes."

The woman picked up the pregnancy test and dragged it across the scanner. Nothing appeared on the screen. She tried again, and again. For some reason, the machine wasn't reading the bar code.

Please don't yell out, Price check on a pregnancy test! George thought, staring anxiously at the woman. Please don't! Even though she'd walked two miles to get to a more out-of-the-way drugstore, there was still a chance George would know someone in the store.

"This thing hasn't been working right all day," the salesclerk muttered. "Just a second while I type this number in." She typed at the cash register for a few seconds. "Sorry to make you wait."

"It's okay," George said. Just hurry!

"I'm sure you're dying to get home and find out whether you can expect a bundle of joy in nine months," the salesclerk said. "Boy, you must be excited. Do you want a boy or a girl?"

"N-neither," George stuttered. That wasn't what she meant—she just wasn't prepared for either! "I mean, um, I don't care."

"That's exactly how I felt, when I had my first," the woman went on. "And what do you know, everyone thought I'd have a girl, but it turned out to be a boy, and—"

George read the price on the cash register and handed her money across the counter. "Sorry, but I really have to go," she said.

"I understand *completely*," the salesclerk said.

No, George thought, I don't think you do! She stuffed her few remaining quarters back into her pocket.

The salesclerk handed her a small brown bag with the pregnancy test inside. "Well, good luck! And thanks for shopping here."

"Thanks," George mumbled. She shoved the small bag into her other coat pocket and ran out the door. Once she was outside, on the sidewalk, George burst into tears.

Just talking to that woman for two minutes had made George realize how serious the situation was! If she was pregnant, she'd have to rethink everything. Her whole life would change.

She wasn't ready for any of this! And it was all her own fault, for sleeping with Will. Maybe *fault* wasn't the right word—but *responsibility* was. Of course, they'd used protection and practiced safe sex. Both George and Will were very careful about using birth control. But George knew that even the most reliable types of birth control weren't a hundred percent guaranteed. There was always a chance you could get pregnant.

If it turned out George wasn't pregnant, she promised herself that she'd never have sex with Will again.

"I don't know if I buy that whole setup," Terry commented to Nancy as they walked out of the Tivoli movie theater Wednesday night. "It wasn't anything like his other films. What did you think? Was it believable?"

Nancy narrowed her eyes at Terry. "That depends. Do you believe that we're all going to live on Mars someday?"

"Hey, I'm up for it," Terry said. "As long as they have VCRs up there."

Nancy laughed. She'd never met anyone as addicted to movies as Terry. He'd seen more movies than she'd even knew existed. Even more impressive, he remembered all the plots. Nancy could barely remember what had happened in the film they'd just seen, but maybe that was because she had other things on her mind. Like the fact that Jake wasn't sitting beside her and the fact that he hadn't even wanted to talk to her that afternoon.

"So what do you think? Is it worth doing a special weekend of all his films on campus?" Terry asked.

"I don't know," Nancy said. "Do you want to get a coffee and talk about it?"

"Sure," Terry said, sounding surprised. "Want to go to Anthony's? We could get something besides popcorn for dinner."

Nancy nodded. "Sounds good, even though the popcorn was delicious."

"And healthy," Terry added. "All that fiber."

Nancy laughed as they started walking down the sidewalk. She took a deep breath, inhaling the pleasant evening air. She loved the smell of fall.

"It's too bad Jake couldn't make it," Terry said as they strolled along the main street, checking out shop windows. "What did you say he had to do again?"

"He had a review session for his history class,"

Nancy said. She glanced sideways at Terry. They were good enough friends that he deserved to know the truth. "But that's not the real reason he didn't come."

"Oh?" Terry asked. "What is? Doesn't he like Marc Bartique movies?"

"That's not it," Nancy said.

"He doesn't like going to the movies?" Terry guessed.

"Not exactly."

Terry nodded. "I get it. He doesn't like going to the movies with *me*."

"Sort of," Nancy said. "Actually, right now he wouldn't want to go to the movies with me, either. We broke up Monday night."

"You're kidding," Terry said.

"No, I'm not," Nancy said. "It just wasn't working out."

Terry stopped walking and turned to face Nancy. He put his hands on her shoulders. "I don't want to sound happy about this. But I am. Because I can't help hoping that now there's a chance for you and me."

Nancy didn't know what to say. She liked Terry, but she'd never thought of him as more than a friend. Although she did feel attracted to him, she was pretty sure it was only because he reminded her of Ned. He certainly wasn't the reason she'd broken up with Jake.

"Look, I know this just happened, and I'm not

trying to pressure you," Terry continued, staring into Nancy's eyes. "But maybe, in a little while, you'll be ready."

"Maybe," Nancy said. "But it's too soon right now."

"I understand," Terry said. "Take all the time you need. I can wait."

"I should be back in an hour or so," Pam said, slinging her knapsack over her shoulder. "Or however long it takes to find the books I need."

"Take all the time you want," George told her. "You don't need to rush back."

Pam put her hands on her hips. "Are you trying to get rid of me or something? Is Will coming over? Do you guys have some hot and heavy date planned?"

"No!" George said. "Nothing like that. I just—"

"Have to work on that paper. Yeah, yeah, I know," Pam said.

"Paper?" George mumbled. "Oh, right! That paper. Yeah. Due tomorrow. It's going to be a killer."

"Well, don't work too hard," Pam said. "See you later!" She closed the door behind her.

"Finally!" George said. She had been waiting for a moment of privacy ever since she got back from the drugstore.

As soon as Pam was gone, George opened her

top desk drawer and dug out the small brown paper bag.

She took the box out of the bag, opened it, and lifted out the sheet of directions. Now all she had to do was take the whole thing down the hall to the bathroom.

As she started reading the directions, there was a loud knock on the door. George crumpled up the paper in her hand. Would she never have any privacy?

She shoved the test back into the box and pushed the box into the back of her desk drawer. Then she leaped up to answer the door. "Hello," she said in an irritated voice as she pulled it open.

Will was standing in the hall. "Hello? Is that the best you can do?"

"Oh, hi," George said. "I didn't know it was you." A mixture of feelings swirled through her. She felt happy, and sad, and—oh, no, mood swings, another symptom listed in that article about pregnancy, George realized. "Come on in," she told Will.

"How are you feeling?" Will asked in a sympathetic tone.

"Feeling?" George repeated. "Fine. I'm fine. Why?"

"Relax," Will said, kissing George on the cheek. "I just wanted to make sure you'd recovered from your flu."

Relax, George thought, forcing herself to

smile. As if she could! "Sorry. I guess I'm kind of on edge. You know, I fell behind in my classes the past couple of days, missing lectures and all that."

"Yeah, I know," Will said. "That's why it kind of surprised me when Andy told me he'd bumped into you at the pharmacy. I know you have work to catch up on. So how come you were doing your laundry?"

"Oh. Well, see . . ." George fumbled for an excuse. Why was everyone suddenly keeping tabs on her? "You know how I felt sick Monday. I was ill Sunday night, too. That's why I didn't do my laundry. And so by the time I felt better today, I didn't have anything to wear, and—look, I haven't seen you in days. Let's not waste our time talking about fabric softener, okay?"

Will shrugged. "Okay. I was just curious, that's all."

"So, we had a date tonight, didn't we?" George said, plastering a fake smile on her face.

"Not officially," Will said. "But I was kind of hoping that since you couldn't go out last night . . ." He trailed his hand down her arm. "You'd have some time tonight."

"Oh, sure. Let's go out," George said. "Better make it a quick dinner, though. I've got tons of work to catch up on."

"You're such a romantic," Will said, hugging her closely to him.

"Mmm," George muttered, her arms hanging limply at her sides. She didn't see any way out of this one.

Ginny gazed across the table at Malcolm. He was wearing a charcoal gray wool blazer over a white shirt and black jeans. A small white candle flickered in a tiny dish, next to a vase of fresh-cut flowers.

Talk about a complete turnaround, Ginny thought. She couldn't get over the contrast between Ray and Malcolm. Where Ray was wild and unpredictable, Malcolm was calm and conventional. He'd been polite and thoughtful all night, ever since they'd left the hospital together. Being with him made Ginny feel like an adult.

"So, do you have a roommate?" Malcolm asked. "Do you live in a single, or—"

"A suite," Ginny said. "And I have a great roommate. Her name's Liz, and she's from New York."

"And how about you? Where did you grow up?" Malcolm asked. "I want to know everything about you." He leaned forward with a seductive smile.

Ginny fiddled with the hem of the tablecloth. Malcolm was seriously interested in her—she couldn't believe it. "I'm from California, the San Francisco area," Ginny said. "My grandparents came from China."

"Cool." Malcolm nodded. "Have you ever been to China?"

"Not since I was little," Ginny said. "I don't remember much. I'd like to go one summer, while I'm still in college."

"And before you get roped into the med school schedule," Malcolm said. "Because once you start, it's impossible to get any time off."

"You sound like you could use a break," Ginny said.

"I could. And I'll get one soon enough, I guess. I mean, once I finish my residency and start my own practice," Malcolm added quickly. "I can't wait. I'm going to buy a house and get rid of my old car, trade it in for a Porsche . . ."

"But won't you have tons of student loans to pay off first?" Ginny asked, sipping her glass of ice water.

The smile on Malcolm's face vanished.

"Sorry!" Ginny said quickly. "I didn't mean to pry. That's your business."

"No, it's okay," Malcolm said. "I just don't like to think about all the debt I'm in."

"And I had to bring it up, right?" Ginny said. "Way to go, Ginny."

"Don't be so hard on yourself," Malcolm said. "Anyone would be curious about that. But you know, Ginny, as bad as it is, sometimes there are other ways to make money. So you don't fall so far behind."

"Like what? Taking a paper route on your way home from a swing shift?" Ginny teased.

Malcolm laughed. "Not exactly. But you have to look for opportunities. Be an entrepreneur. Play your cards right."

"Spend spring break in Vegas?" Ginny suggested, her lips curling into a smile. "Well, it's not the most traditional route through med school, but—"

"You're funny," Malcolm said. "In fact, you're so funny I keep forgetting how beautiful you are." He leaned across the small corner table and kissed Ginny.

She kissed him back, with a delirious feeling that she was floating. She sat back and looked at Malcolm. For a few seconds she'd forgotten that they were sitting in a crowded restaurant.

"Look, Ginny. I know I probably wasn't supposed to do that. I mean, you're a volunteer, I'm a doctor, and I've only known you a few days," Malcolm said in a soft voice. "But I already feel so close to you."

"I feel the same way about you," Ginny said. She hadn't kissed anyone since Ray, and she'd been afraid it would feel strange, or unnatural. Instead, it felt wonderful.

Malcolm is here now, she reminded herself. *Malcolm is the present. Ray is the past.*

Looking across the table at Malcolm, that was exactly the way Ginny wanted things to stay.

CHAPTER 6

Will held George's hand as they strolled across campus after dinner at Souvlaki House. Will was glad to see that George had her appetite back. She had eaten a large Greek salad and a bowl of soup as well.

"Now that you're feeling healthy again," Will began, "maybe you could come over and stay at my place tonight."

"Tonight?" George asked.

Will squeezed her hand. "Well, sure, tonight. George, we haven't spent the night together in over a week. Don't you miss me as much as I miss you?"

"Isn't that **a c**ountry-western song?" George joked.

"I'm serious," Will said. He stopped walking

and turned to her. "Come on, George. Let's go back to my place, watch a movie, cuddle—"

"I'd love to," George said.

"Great! Let's—"

"But I have a headache," George said. "A really bad headache. Pounding." She rubbed her temples.

"I have aspirin," Will offered.

"I can't take aspirin. It upsets my stomach," George said, shaking her head.

"Okay. Well, I could give you a neck massage, and that sometimes helps headaches," Will offered, touching her lightly on the neck. "Or I could kiss it away . . ."

"It's not just the headache," George said, stepping out of his reach. "I've got all my homework to catch up on, and I need to borrow Pam's notes, and she's going to be home in half an hour, so I need to meet her and—"

Will took a step backward. "Why do I get the feeling you're not going to come over, no matter what I say? Are you avoiding me?"

"Well, n-no," George stammered. "I'm really busy, that's all."

"George, we're all busy. All the time. That doesn't mean we can't make time for each other," Will said. "It's called having a serious relationship."

George bit her lip, looking over Will's shoulder. "Maybe I'm not ready for a serious relationship right now."

"What?" Will couldn't believe what he was hearing. "But, George, you're already *in* one. We've been seeing each other for weeks."

"Then I guess I need a break," George said, looking uncomfortable.

"A break?" Will asked. He felt like an idiot, repeating everything she said. But he was so stunned, he couldn't come up with another response. He looked at George. Why was she doing this? Hadn't they been getting along as well as they always did?

"Some space. You know," George said, putting her hand on Will's arm. "A chance to catch my breath and focus on other things."

"Other things? Like what?" Will asked.

"School. Friends," George explained. "I need a little more time to myself. I'll see you."

"When?" Will asked, as George turned to walk away.

"I'll call you!" George called over her shoulder.

"When?" Will shouted after her.

"Soon!" George yelled.

Will's shoulders slumped. George might as well have said never. That was what she meant.

He didn't understand what was going on. Why did George suddenly want so much space between them? Had he done something wrong?

* * *

"I had a great time," Ginny said, opening the door to get out of Malcolm's car. He had pulled up alongside Thayer, in the parking lot.

"So did I," Malcolm said. "Hold on a second, Ginny—don't go yet."

"I've got to," Ginny said. "Not to sound like my mother, but it's a school night, and I still have a few hours of homework to do."

"Man! Your schedule's even worse than mine," Malcolm said.

"Sometimes it seems like it," Ginny said. "But I figure if I do well this year, in all my premed classes, I'll be set up for the future."

"Ginny, grades aren't everything, you know. Just remember that," Malcolm said, sounding very serious all of a sudden.

Ginny's eyebrows creased. "What do you mean?"

"Just, well, you can get the best grades there are, and still not end up at the med school you wanted or doing the kind of work you pictured," Malcolm said, rubbing his thumb against the steering wheel.

Ginny stared at his face. He looked angry, and she wondered whether that was what had happened to him. But that didn't make sense—he was at a great hospital, working with one of the best specialists in the country. "No, I know," Ginny said. "And believe me, I have other interests besides medicine."

"Like?" Malcolm turned to her with a smile.

"Like music. I've written some songs for a rock band," Ginny confessed.

"You know what?" Malcolm reached over, putting his hand on Ginny's cheek. "You're full of surprises."

Ginny shrugged, embarrassed by Malcolm's attention. "I try."

"So do you have any other . . . interests?" Malcolm leaned across the seat and kissed Ginny, running his hand through her long, black hair.

"You mean, like you?" Ginny smiled, then returned Malcolm's kiss. At the moment she couldn't think of anything or anyone she was more interested in than Malcolm.

"That would be nice," Malcolm said.

"I'm definitely interested," Ginny told him. "But that doesn't change the fact that I have to get upstairs and finish my chem assignment. So, good night."

"See you tomorrow at the lab," Malcolm said.

As Ginny took the steps up to the third floor, she felt as if she were flying.

George drummed her fingers against her desk. She'd been waiting for Pam to leave for her Thursday morning class since seven o'clock, when she woke up. So far, Pam had tried on six different outfits, and she wasn't dressed yet.

George stood up and started pacing around the

room, every now and then shooting irritated glances at Pam, hoping she'd take the hint and get going.

"Having trouble with your paper?" Pam asked, leaning over to tie her shoelaces.

"No," George muttered through clenched teeth.

"You're not? You seem kind of upset," Pam commented. "Everything okay?"

"Sure. But it's really hard to concentrate in here, with you getting ready," George snapped.

Pam raised her eyebrows. "So go to the library, that's what it's for."

"I don't *feel* like going to the library," George replied coldly.

"I'll be gone in a second," Pam said. "If you're going to be this grumpy, I don't want to hang around, believe me." She stood up and stuffed her comb into her backpack. Then she walked out the door, slamming it behind her. Finally.

George opened her desk drawer and dug out the small box. It's now or never, George told herself as she headed down the hall to the bathroom.

"You would have been *so* proud of me," Stephanie said, closing the door behind her. It was the first time she had seen Casey since her acting triumph Wednesday afternoon.

"Wait—don't tell me. You were actually nice

to your stepmother on the phone," Casey guessed.

"No." Stephanie's disagreements with her father's new wife, Kiki, were legendary. But Stephanie didn't plan on being nice to her any time soon.

She tossed her scarf in Casey's direction as she walked to her closet to pick out an outfit for her afternoon shift at Berrigan's. "I've been working on my plan to kidnap Jonathan. And yesterday I snowed the store manager into giving us both Saturday off."

"You're kidding," Casey said. "What did you tell him?"

"That my grandmother's heart was . . ." Stephanie pretended to start crying. "Just not the same anymore! In fact, it might give out any second!"

"Please. That's the oldest story in the world," Casey said, shaking her head. "And he actually bought it?"

Stephanie held her head high. "What can I say. I'm a very convincing actress. In fact, I'm thinking about trying out for *Cat on a Hot Tin Roof* next week."

"Yeah, right. More like *Cat Who Wants to Get Out of Town for the Weekend,*" Casey said. "Just how thick did you pour it on?"

"All I can say is, you'd better look out. You're not the only actor in Suite 301," Stephanie warned.

"Right," Casey said. "So, where are you guys going anyway?"

"I don't know yet. I have to make some calls," Stephanie said. "I was thinking a romantic, quiet bed and breakfast in a small town. Know any?"

"I've got a guidebook for B and B's in the area," Casey volunteered, going over to her bookshelf. "I bought it when Charley was coming to visit the first time. I flagged some of the places I thought sounded interesting. I'll show you." She sat down on Stephanie's bed.

"You mean you don't trust me to pick a place by myself?" Stephanie said.

"Just thought I'd help. Don't forget you can't afford the Plaza in New York. Or the Chicago Hilton."

"Please, I know I'm on a budget now," Stephanie said, sitting down beside Casey. "Anyway, my sick grandmother doesn't live anywhere near there." She grinned.

Bess was sitting on a wooden bench in the middle of the Lawn. She'd just gotten out of her last Friday class. It was a gorgeous sunny afternoon— the sky was clear and the air was crisp. Bess closed her eyes and tilted her face to the sun. She felt terrific. She couldn't wait for the weekend to start.

"Bess! Bess!"

Bess put her hand over her eyebrows, shading

her eyes from the bright sunlight. Somebody was running toward her, but she couldn't make out who, because of the glare.

Suddenly the figure came into view. It was Ned!

Bess jumped off the bench just in time to throw her arms around Ned's shoulders, welcoming him with an enthusiastic hug.

"Bess, it's so good to see you," Ned whispered into her ear. "I've missed you so much."

Bess felt a tingle run up her spine as Ned held her close. "You, too," she said softly, her cheek pressed against his soft plaid flannel shirt.

Ned stepped back and looked Bess squarely in the eye. Then he tipped her chin with his fingers and leaned forward, pressing his lips to hers. Bess put her hands on Ned's shoulders, leaning into the kiss. She hadn't felt so alive in a long time.

All of a sudden, Ned was tugging on her arm. "What? What is it?" Bess asked, wrestling out of his grasp.

"It's time to get up," Leslie King replied, snapping off the alarm clock beside Bess's bed. "If you press the snooze button one more time, it's going to fall off. Or I'm going to break it!"

Bess blinked a few times and opened her eyes. "Did you just shake my arm?"

Leslie nodded. "You're going to be late to class if you don't hustle."

"So . . . wait. This is Thursday?" Bess asked, confused.

Leslie tossed Bess's terry robe onto her bed, where it landed on Bess's face. "Take a shower and snap out of it!" she said.

George stared at her watch. She'd set the stopwatch function to five minutes. She was starting to wonder if her watch was broken—the seconds were ticking away so slowly, it was unreal.

She'd set the small plastic test unit on a tissue on top of her dresser. She wasn't going to look at it until the five minutes were up. No matter how much the suspense was killing her.

She stood up and walked over to the window. Gazing out at the pretty Wilder campus, as students changed classes, filing back and forth across the quad, it was hard to believe how tense she felt.

Suddenly the stopwatch beeped. George was so startled, she nearly jumped through the ceiling. She took a deep breath and turned around, facing her dresser.

If the little white patch in the middle of the plastic unit turned pink, that meant George was pregnant. If it was blue, then she wasn't pregnant.

George's hand shook as she lifted the test to get a close look at it. The patch wasn't pink. But it wasn't blue, either.

It was lavender—a mix of the two! What was

that supposed to indicate? She picked up the directions and studied them again. "For occasional inconclusive results, which occur in only two percent of all cases, please see your doctor, or purchase another test and try again."

George tossed the plastic stick into the trash can. "Try again? It took me a whole day just to take this one!"

"Any new ideas for a story hit you yet?" Gail asked when Nancy walked into the *Wilder Times* office on Friday morning for a staff meeting. So far, Gary Friedman, Gail, and Jake were the only ones present.

"Not exactly." Nancy frowned and took a seat across the table from Jake. "I've been trying really hard, but I haven't come up with a thing."

"Hmm. Must be something that's going around," Gail said. She glanced pointedly at Jake.

"Writer's block is contagious, you know," Gary commented.

"It is?" Nancy tried to smile.

"Sure," Gary said. "It hits entire blocks at the same time."

Jake groaned. "It's bad enough not having an idea, without having to listen to really bad puns, too."

Nancy felt a smile curl the corners of her

mouth. Despite how angry she felt at Jake, he could still make her laugh.

"I don't know what the problem is," Gary commented, putting his feet on the table. "You've got an assignment—a dream assignment. Kissing all over campus—"

"Forget it, Friedman. That's off. We're not a *couple* anymore, okay?" Jake interrupted harshly.

"Gee. Sorry!" Gary said. "I didn't know."

"Well, pay attention," Jake said.

"Some of us have better things to do than keep track of your love life, Collins," Gary said. He was quiet for a moment. "You know, if you *wanted* to get back together, that story might be the way to do it—"

"Forget it. I'm out of here," Jake said, standing.

"You can't leave," Gail instructed him. "You walked out on the last staff meeting, remember?"

"Then *I'll* go," Nancy said, getting to her feet.

"You don't have to," Jake told her.

"No, really—it's my pleasure." Nancy grabbed her backpack and slung it over her shoulder, heading for the door.

"You still need to come up with a story idea by Monday!" Gail called after her as she went out into the hall.

Nancy leaned against the wall and sighed. Why did she feel that quitting the newspaper might be the best thing she could do right then? If Jake was going to be a jerk to her every time she showed up at the office, what was the point?

But I didn't join the *Wilder Times* for Jake. I joined it because I want to be a reporter. I just have to find a story.

Ginny walked down the hall of the hospital Friday morning, carrying a new box of slides from the supply room to the lab. She and Malcolm had been working side by side for the last two hours.

Malcolm was studying and categorizing blood samples taken from patients who were being treated with the new heart medication, Alpha II, and from patients who weren't using the drug. Ginny had been helping him sort through the slides and organize the data. We really do make a great team, she thought, walking back into the lab.

Ginny paused in the doorway to look at Malcolm sitting at his desk, hunched over his work. He was so serious and so dedicated. All those stories about doctors being selfish didn't apply to him at all. Ginny only hoped she'd be the same way when she was in the middle of her own residency.

In the past week, thanks to Malcolm, she'd gone from feeling undecided about her premed major to being more and more committed to it.

Malcolm was helping so many people, just as Ginny hoped to.

She set the box of slides down on a table and tiptoed quietly up to Malcolm to surprise him with a hug. She reached forward to put her hands over his eyes.

Malcolm was peeling a tiny white label off one slide from the "Treated" side of the desk. He then stuck the label on a slide from the "Untreated" side of the desk. The labels had numbers on them that identified each patient; the results were tracked by these patient numbers. So why was Malcolm changing the numbers around? Had she made a mistake—done something wrong, something that could ruin the whole project?

Ginny sucked in her breath as Malcolm repeated the process.

Malcolm's shoulders twitched, and he dropped one of the slides. "Ginny!" he cried, looking over his shoulder as the glass slide clattered on the desk. "You scared me."

"Sorry," Ginny said. "I wasn't trying to sneak up on you."

"Oh, no? Then what were you doing?" Malcolm asked with a flirtatious lilt to his voice.

"I was going to surprise you, but then I saw you labeling the slides and I—I didn't want to interrupt you," Ginny told him, her voice shaky with nervousness. "I didn't do something wrong, did I? When I was labeling the slides earlier?"

"No, *I* did," Malcolm said. "While you were gone, I guess I wasn't paying attention. All of a sudden, I realized I'd been doing everything backward." He shook his head. "The absent-minded professor thing. So I had to change all the ones I'd just done."

"Oh." Ginny nodded. "I get it. Wow, I can't believe this."

"Believe what?" Malcolm asked.

"You actually made a mistake, Malcolm. It means you're human!" Ginny teased.

"It *means* I didn't have my best lab assistant when I needed her," Malcolm said, pulling Ginny onto his lap. He picked up a length of her shiny black hair and ran his fingers through it. "My beautiful lab assistant." Ginny leaned back as Malcolm rubbed her neck. "In fact, maybe I should see about hiring you full-time."

"Forget it," Ginny said.

"Forget it?" Malcolm asked. "Aren't you as crazy about me as I am about you?"

"Of course," Ginny said. "But didn't you tell me it's not such a good idea for us to see each other?" She traced small circles on Malcolm's chest.

"Forget what I said. Forget we're even at the hospital," Malcolm whispered in her ear. He pulled her closer and kissed her again.

With Malcolm kissing her, Ginny found it easy to forget almost everything.

*　　*　　*

"Stephanie, we should get going!" Jonathan yelled over the loud music at the Underground Friday night. "I have to be at work tomorrow at nine!"

Stephanie smiled. No, you don't! she thought. Because she had already arranged for Jonathan to have the whole weekend off—without his knowing about it.

No, tomorrow morning Jonathan would be waking up in a small, romantic bed and breakfast in Spring Green, Wisconsin. But he didn't need to know that yet.

She jingled the key to the rental car in her pocket. "Well, if you really think we should leave," she said, pouting. "I was having such a good time!"

"I know. I'm sorry. My schedule's lousy. It always gets in the way, doesn't it?" Jonathan gently guided her toward the door of the cafeteria that was transformed into an on-campus club on weekend nights.

Not always! Stephanie thought. "Maybe you could try to get a day off sometime soon," she said sadly. "I feel as if we never see each other."

"I'll try," Jonathan said. "But I don't know if I can." He stopped, putting his arms around Stephanie's waist. "Hey, why don't you come home with me? We could at least spend a little more time together."

"I don't know," Stephanie said.

"Come on," Jonathan urged. "Please?"

"Well, okay," Stephanie said. "I've got to run home first and grab a few things, but I'll be over in half an hour."

"I'll come with you," Jonathan said.

"Oh, no, you don't have to," Stephanie said. "It's just . . . my toothbrush. I think I can carry it."

"All right. But hurry," Jonathan said. "We don't have much time."

Stephanie smiled, waving goodbye. That's what you think!

CHAPTER 7

"Why isn't there ever anything good on TV on Friday night?" Nancy asked, turning to Ginny and Liz. The three of them were sprawled out in the lounge of their suite at about nine o'clock.

Nancy stretched her legs out on the couch. She wouldn't admit it to anyone, but she was hanging around the dorm because she was expecting Ned to call. If he left Emerson after his last class, he ought to be in Weston by now. So why hadn't he called?

"There's a law against good TV on Friday nights," Liz said, pressing the remote, "because we're not supposed to stay in on Friday night."

"Hey, it's not by choice," Ginny said. "Can I help it if Malcolm is on rotation tonight?"

"Malcolm, is he the doctor you're seeing?" Nancy asked.

Ginny nodded.

"You should see him, Nancy. He's a *hunk,*" Liz said. "He should be on one of those TV series about doctors. He's better looking than any of the actors."

Nancy laughed. "Really? Wow!"

The telephone in Nancy's room started ringing. Nancy jumped up and ran to answer it. Ned— finally! "Hello?" she said eagerly.

"Nancy! I'm so glad I caught you," Carson Drew's deep voice replied.

"Oh, hi, Dad," Nancy said, trying not to sound too disappointed. "What's up?"

"Not much. I just wanted to say hello," he said. "I'm going to be in and out tomorrow, and I was afraid I'd miss talking to you over the weekend. So, how are things?"

Not too great, Nancy thought. She could tell her father about breaking up with Jake or her confused feelings for Ned. She could tell him anything. They were very close. But right now, she didn't feel like talking in case Ned tried to call.

"Dad, I'd love to chat, but the thing is, I was just on my way out," Nancy said.

"Oh, really? Of course, it's Friday night. I forgot." Carson laughed. "Doing something fun, I hope?"

"Oh, yeah. I'm, uh, meeting Bess and George,"

Nancy said quickly. "And I'd better run. I was literally halfway out the door when you called."

"My timing's lousy, as usual," her father said. "Well, give me a call Sunday, okay?"

"Sure. Thanks, Dad. Bye!" Nancy hung up the phone, feeling slightly guilty. She wasn't trying to avoid her father. It was just that she wanted to see Ned. She couldn't explain why it was so important to her. Maybe because everything in her life had changed so much, she wanted to talk about it with Ned. He knew her better than anybody.

"Who was that?" Liz asked as Nancy walked back into the lounge.

"My dad," Nancy answered.

Just as Nancy was settling back onto the couch, the front door to the suite opened, and Stephanie swept into the room. "Well, if it isn't the Stay at Home Club," she said. "What are you watching—'One Hundred and One Ways to Knit'?"

Liz looked at her and raised an eyebrow. "And I suppose you were in New York City for the evening. You just flew back for an hour to share the details with us, right?"

Ginny laughed. "No, not New York. Paris."

Stephanie sat on the arm of a large easy chair. "Ha-ha. You two are hilarious. Actually, I managed to have fun right here in Weston, if you can believe that. Personally, I think it strains the limits of the imagination."

Nancy shook her head. Stephanie had been

pulling her snob act ever since she'd moved into their suite. They were all so used to it that, for the most part, they ignored her.

"I was at the Underground, with Jonathan," Stephanie announced. "I had such a great time dancing. The music was even good."

"So why did you leave?" Liz asked. "Surely not to come back here and share your joy with *us?*"

Stephanie looked at her as if she were crazy. "No way. I came back to get a change of clothes. I'm taking Jonathan on a trip this weekend, out of town."

"Hmm. Well, that's one way to stay away from other guys," Liz commented wryly.

"I'm not seeing any other guys," Stephanie said, sounding offended. "Not anymore. I'm in love with Jonathan. I'm committed to him. And if you were as happy as I am right now, you wouldn't feel the need to snipe at me," Stephanie declared. "Hey, speaking of being in love, what's the deal with Ned and Bess? I didn't know they were dating."

"Ned and Bess?" Nancy asked. "They're not."

"Then how come I just saw them at the Underground together, dancing about two inches apart?" Stephanie asked.

So Ned *was* in town already. And he hadn't called Nancy. What was he doing? Was there something going on with him and Bess that Nancy didn't know about?

* * *

95

"I've got to take a break," Bess told Ned. She tugged at his sleeve, pulling him over to a quiet table at the back of the room. "I haven't danced this much since . . ."

"I know," Ned said, wrapping an arm around Bess's shoulders and giving her a quick squeeze. "Since Paul. Sorry, I didn't mean to make you stay out there so long."

"It's not your fault," Bess said, sliding into a seat. "I wanted to dance. Really. That felt good. I just didn't realize how out of shape I've gotten." She smiled wanly.

"Yeah, well. Sitting around reading fashion mags will do that to you," Ned said knowingly.

"Ooh. Using private confessions *against* me," Bess said, shaking her head. "How could you!"

Ned laughed. "Sorry. It won't happen again."

Bess smiled at him. She'd been having such a nice time with Ned since he'd shown up that afternoon. They'd talked over a long, relaxing dinner at a restaurant outside of town. Bess had told Ned about feeling left out of social events lately, so he'd insisted on going to the Underground with her, as a way of getting her back into the swing of things.

"Hey, maybe we should call Nancy and George," Bess suggested. "Make this a real party."

Ned shook his head. "Let's not."

Bess was surprised. Even though Ned and

Nancy didn't go out anymore, she knew they still cared about each other.

Ned sighed. "You know, Bess, I feel like I'm finally over Nancy. It took a long time. And if I see her right now—well, maybe I won't feel the same way."

"You're afraid seeing her might stir up some old feelings?" Bess asked.

"Exactly," Ned said. "And, anyway, I didn't come here to visit Nancy. I came to see *you.*"

"Oh." Bess felt her face turn a little pink. "Well, thanks."

"Don't thank me," Ned said. "Not to sound like a cliché, but that *is* what friends are for. Hey, speaking of which, what about George? How's she doing? You haven't mentioned her."

"I don't really know how she's doing," Bess said. "I haven't seen her in a couple of days. The last time I did, she was feeling really sick. Like, nauseated sick, and she looked sort of green."

"Too bad," Ned said.

"Yeah, I should call her. If she's feeling better, maybe the three of us could go out to breakfast tomorrow," Bess suggested.

"Definitely. I've been thinking about the blueberry buckwheat pancakes at the Bumblebee Diner since the last time I was in town," Ned said.

Bess raised an eyebrow at him. "The social life *is* dull at Emerson, isn't it?"

*   *   *

George sat by the telephone in her room on Friday night. She wanted to call somebody. She desperately needed to talk to someone about all the feelings she was having. But who could she confide in?

Her parents? No way. Out of the question.

Pam was gone for the weekend. Which was a good thing, considering how tense the atmosphere in their room had been lately.

She'd tried Bess's room, but Leslie had answered. She told George that Bess and Ned were out dancing at the Underground. George was glad her friend had gone out, but she couldn't help wishing Bess had stayed in just *one* more night.

Nancy was no doubt out with Ned and Bess.

That left Will. Why can't I call Will? George asked herself. Because I don't know what I'll do if it turns out I'm pregnant. Her period was now a whole week late. It had never been that late before. She didn't know why she was going to bother with another test tomorrow morning, Saturday, but that was her plan.

Nancy opened her closet door and took out a pair of black jeans and a black- and white-checked blouse. She changed quickly, slipping into her black leather boots—her favorite shoes to dance in. She'd had enough bad TV—she wanted to go out and celebrate the end of the week!

Ned probably tried to call and couldn't get

through, Nancy decided. Kara had been on the phone for a while earlier in the evening. Well, Nancy would just catch up with Ned and Bess. As she ran a brush through her hair, she checked her makeup in the mirror over her dresser.

On second thought, why should she go to the Underground alone?

She picked up the phone and dialed as she stuffed a few dollars into her purse. "Hi, Terry? It's Nancy. Hey, do you feel like going out tonight?"

"Come on, Bess. One last dance," Ned said, holding out his hand.

Bess let him pull her to her feet. Then she reached up and clasped her hands behind his neck. Swaying back and forth across the crowded dance floor, Bess couldn't help remembering the first time she'd danced with Paul, at a Zeta party. He had held her almost exactly the same way.

She rested her head on Ned's shoulder so he wouldn't see the tears in her eyes. Then she spotted Nancy walking in. Bess wiped her eyes and was about to wave her over when she spotted Terry standing behind Nancy.

Terry? What was he doing with her? She'd only broken up with Jake a couple of days ago.

Bess remembered what Ned had said earlier, about not wanting to see Nancy because it might make him have feelings for her again. Seeing

Nancy with Terry would only make him feel worse.

She had to get Ned away from the door. "Come on, Ned—it's too crowded here," she said. "Let's head for the other side of the room."

Nancy paused in the doorway, scanning the crowded dance floor. She didn't see Ned and Bess anywhere. They must have left already, she thought. Well, that didn't mean she couldn't have fun. She and Terry could still make a night of it.

"Want to dance?" Terry asked.

"Definitely," Nancy said. She stepped onto the edge of the dance floor, and Terry put his arms around her. Together they moved to the center of the floor.

That was when Nancy spotted Bess. She and Ned were dancing, too. Ned was holding Bess close, his hands on her back.

Stephanie was right, Nancy thought, trying to catch her breath. They *are* on a date!

She didn't know whether to feel furious or sad. All she knew was that she'd never felt more jealous in her entire life.

She moved closer to Terry, pressing her face to his shoulder. Just then the song ended. Bess and Ned stopped dancing and separated. Ned looked around the dance floor.

His gaze met Nancy's. When he saw her with Terry, his eyes widened in surprise.

Nancy turned away quickly. She couldn't bear to see him with his arms around one of her best friends.

"Good song, huh?" Terry said, staring deeply into Nancy's eyes. He ran his hand down her back.

Nancy nodded. Then, without even thinking about what she was doing, she leaned forward and kissed Terry on the lips.

If he was surprised, he didn't show it. He kissed her back, holding her tightly. Neither one of them moved for a minute, even though a new, fast song had started, and people were dancing all around them to a heavy drumbeat.

When they finally separated, Terry looked stunned. Nancy didn't know what to say. The last thing she'd planned to do when she asked him to go out was kiss him. But she'd felt so jealous, she'd have done anything to make Ned feel as bad as she did.

"So, um, how about getting something to drink?" Nancy suggested, trying to break the awkward silence.

"Sounds good," Terry said, nodding.

Nancy glanced around the Underground as they went to the snack bar. She didn't see Bess, or Ned, anywhere.

CHAPTER 8

At ten o'clock Ginny walked down the hall toward the research lab. She'd taken a cab over to meet Malcolm, after he called to see if they could go out for coffee when he got off work. Maybe it won't be such a boring Friday night after all, Ginny thought with a smile, quietly pushing open the door.

Malcolm was sitting at his desk in the far corner, and Ginny could hear that he was on the telephone.

"Louis, I told you," Malcolm said. "Everything's under control. Don't worry."

Ginny didn't mean to eavesdrop. She sneaked back outside, but that floor of the hospital was so quiet at night, she could still hear every word. Malcolm had raised his voice as if he were upset.

"Louis, look. How many times do we have to

go over this?" Malcolm went on. "No one's ever going to hear anything about Alpha Two and any liver damage." He paused for a minute. "Because I'll make sure they don't, that's why."

Liver damage? What was Malcolm talking about? Ginny wondered. Since when did liver damage have anything to do with the drug Malcolm was testing? And if it did, why was he keeping it a secret?

"Your job is to take care of things there. My job is to take care of the Alpha results. And I will. End of story! So stop interfering. Everything's going to work out."

Ginny stood in the hallway, her heart pounding. Why did Malcolm sound so angry all of a sudden? And what did he mean by taking care of the results?

A picture of Malcolm changing the labels on the slides flashed through Ginny's mind.

"Okay, we'll talk again tomorrow." There was a loud click as Malcolm hung up the phone.

Ginny took a deep breath, trying to calm herself. Maybe there was a logical explanation for all this. There had to be. This was a well-known hospital, and the project was being run by a top-notch doctor. Obviously there was something Ginny didn't understand.

She pushed open the door. "Malcolm?" she called out.

"Ginny!" Malcolm replied. He leaned over,

locking his file cabinet. "Boy, am I ready to get out of here." He stood up and started walking toward her.

"Long day, huh?" Ginny asked.

Malcolm glanced at his watch. "Let's see. I started at six in the morning, and now it's ten at night. Yeah, you could say it was a long day. I'm ready for some serious downtime." He reached for Ginny's hand. "How about you?"

"Me? I'm ready for anything," Ginny said, squeezing his hand. "I, um, thought I heard you on the phone when I came in. Who's Louis?"

Malcolm's eyes narrowed.

"I didn't mean to—"

"Oh, no. It's okay," Malcolm said. He frowned. "Louis is one of the medical monitors for the Alpha Two project. He checks in on a regular basis."

"Medical monitor? What's that?" Ginny asked.

"Every time a drug's in clinical trials, as Alpha Two is, people like Louis monitor the project. They check the data, make sure everything's on the up-and-up, stuff like that," Malcolm explained.

"So does Louis come in here? Or do you just talk on the phone?" Ginny asked.

"So many questions . . ." Malcolm ran his hand through Ginny's hair. "Don't you want to get out of here?"

"Oh. Yeah, of course," Ginny said. "But you

know me. I'm trying to learn as much as I can about hospital procedure while I'm here."

"Well, trust me, Ginny. Medical monitors are about the most boring part. Just picture what it's like to have someone read the newspaper over your shoulder. That's what they do. Full-time," Malcolm said with an exaggerated grimace.

"Oh." Ginny laughed. "So I shouldn't be signing up for that job?"

"Not unless you want to be as boring as Louis." Malcolm patted his mouth, pretending to yawn. "Yes, Louis. No, Louis. Et cetera."

"Is he really that boring? How come I haven't met him?" Ginny asked.

"Because I've been kind enough to spare you, that's why." Malcolm put his arm around Ginny's shoulders. "Now come on, let's get going."

"Okay," Ginny said. "I can't wait to show you Java Joe's."

As Malcolm took off his lab coat and shut off all the lights, Ginny thought about what she'd overheard. Malcolm had told Louis that everything was under control, and that he'd take care of things, if Louis would only stop interfering. Were medical monitors really that bothersome? It seemed hard to imagine.

But it wasn't as if Malcolm would lie about it. Besides, Malcolm was dedicated and loyal—look at all the hours he put in, even when he wasn't scheduled. But what liver damage was he talking about? If it was connected to the new drug, shouldn't Malcolm tell everyone about it? Wouldn't they find out eventually anyway?

Malcolm put his arm around Ginny as they walked down the hall toward the elevator. "So, tell me about your day. I'm sure it was much more interesting than mine."

Ginny looked at Malcolm. He was kind, considerate, wonderful—so why did Ginny feel that he was lying to her all of a sudden?

"So, did you get your toothbrush?" Jonathan asked, opening the door to let Stephanie into his house.

"I did. But then I realized I didn't have any toothpaste," Stephanie said.

"That's okay. I do," Jonathan said with a laugh. "Come on in."

"I can't. See, I have to go shopping. Because when I realized I was out of toothpaste, I also realized I was out of shampoo, and conditioner, and moisturizer—"

"Which you can buy tomorrow," Jonathan pointed out.

"No, I can't. Come on, will you go with me? Please?" Stephanie asked. "I've got a car and—"

"Now?" Jonathan laughed. "And since when do you have a car?"

"I borrowed it. From Casey. I have to go to the supermarket, and I need you to come with me," Stephanie said. Just a little white lie—it wouldn't hurt anybody. Neither would the fact that Stephanie had packed a suitcase for Jonathan the night before, while he was cooking dinner for them.

"Stephanie, it's the middle of the night. And you want to go grocery shopping?" Jonathan asked. "You hate grocery shopping. You always try to get me to go. That is, if you're not having things delivered."

"That was the old me. This is the new me." Stephanie tugged on his sleeve. "Come on. This is the only time I'm going to get Casey's car, and I have a whole bunch of stuff to buy that's really, really heavy. I want to stock up on soda, and— Well, if you don't want to help me carry it all, I guess I can ask the stock boy—"

"All right, all right!" Jonathan finally relented. "I'll go with you. As long as we're coming back here afterward."

"Of course we're coming back here," Stephanie said with a smile. Just not until Sunday, that's all.

She ushered Jonathan down to the curb and watched as he got into the passenger seat. She got back into the car and started the engine, which automatically locked the doors.

"Trying to make sure I don't jump out and leave you to push the grocery cart all by yourself?" Jonathan joked.

"Something like that," Stephanie said as she pulled the car away from the curb. She quickly headed through town, then made a left onto a county highway.

"Steph? Which store are you going to?" Jonathan asked. "Didn't you want to stop back there?"

"Well, this is kind of a . . . specialty shop," Stephanie told him. "It's got really amazing cheese." She turned toward him. "And it's in Wisconsin."

"Thanks for a terrific night," Terry said, standing outside Nancy's suite in Thayer. "A little on the short side but definitely terrific." He kissed Nancy lightly on the lips. "You are some dancer."

"You, too," Nancy said uneasily. Ever since she'd kissed Terry so boldly on the dance floor, she'd been uncomfortable. It wasn't that she hadn't enjoyed it. She had . . . sort of. But her motive for doing it wasn't something she was proud of.

"I was pretty surprised when you called. But I guess it was only a matter of time before you realized how wonderful I am," Terry said, teasing her.

Nancy nodded.

"So you changed your mind? It's not too

soon?" Terry asked, his voice eager. "You're ready for me?"

Nancy peered into his eyes. On one hand, she wasn't sure if she was ready for another boyfriend. On the other hand, Ned had moved on to Bess. So maybe it was time for Nancy to move on, too. "Listen, Terry. I'm sorry if I've been indecisive," she began.

"Uh-oh," Terry said, backing away. "This doesn't sound good."

"Hold on," Nancy said with a laugh. "What I'm trying to say is, I'd love to go out with you."

"You would?" Terry said with surprise.

"Yes. Why is that such a shock?" Nancy asked. "Isn't that what you wanted me to say?"

"Of course," Terry said. He leaned down to give Nancy a deep kiss. "Good night. And I'll call you tomorrow, okay?"

Nancy nodded. "Sure. Good night." She opened the door and slipped inside, then flopped down on the couch in the lounge. What a night! What had she gotten herself into? She liked Terry, and she was attracted to him. But she knew she'd decided to go out with him for all the wrong reasons.

Bess sat up in bed, her pulse racing. She banged the snooze button on her alarm clock. Why wouldn't it shut off? Then she realized the ringing was the telephone beside her bed.

Bess picked up the phone. "Hello?" she mumbled, her voice groggy.

"Bess! Oh, I'm so glad you're there."

"George?" Bess squinted at her alarm clock. "George, it's seven o'clock. On a Saturday. Where else would I be?"

"I know. I've been waiting since four o'clock to call you," George said breathlessly.

Bess heard a groan and glanced at the floor, where Ned was rolling over in his sleeping bag.

"Since four A.M.?" Bess asked. "Why?"

"I couldn't sleep," George said. "I need to talk to you. Can you meet me for breakfast?"

"Sure. How does ten o'clock sound?" Bess asked. After the Underground, she and Ned had stayed up until two talking. She was exhausted.

"Not ten," George said. "Now. I need to see you now."

"Hungry, huh? Well, okay, I guess." She didn't like the tone of George's voice. She sounded frantic, almost. "George, is everything all right?"

"I'll tell you when I see you," George said. "Meet me at the Cave in an hour, okay?"

"I can do that," Bess said. "Hey, you know Ned's visiting. Can he come to breakfast, too?" Bess asked.

"No!" George practically screamed. "This is private. See you at eight."

"What was that all about?" Ned asked, yawning.

"George needs to see me." Bess swept off her covers and swung her feet onto the carpet. She rubbed her eyes. "It sounds important. I guess I'll meet up with you afterward."

"Fine," Ned mumbled, rolling over and snuggling deeper into his sleeping bag.

Bess looked at Ned sleeping peacefully for a minute. It was hard to believe how angry and upset he'd been the night before, after seeing Nancy with Terry Schneider.

Bess had tried to explain to Ned what had been going on in Nancy's life lately—how she had broken up with Jake on Monday, and how Terry was interested in dating her. But one thing she couldn't explain to Ned was why Nancy was *kissing* Terry. According to Nancy, she wasn't interested in him.

Bess grabbed some clothes from her closet. She could take a shower and then change in the bathroom without bothering Ned and Leslie. She yawned, wondering what was going on with George that could be so urgent.

In the research lab on Saturday morning, Ginny slipped the small key out of Malcolm's top desk drawer. Then she cautiously opened the locked file cabinet where he kept the patient records on Alpha II.

She couldn't believe what she was doing. She had no idea what she was looking for. And she didn't even know if she'd be able to make sense of whatever she found.

All she knew was that since the night before, she had had a vague, uneasy feeling about Malcolm. As if he were hiding something. If Louis was monitoring the project, why *hadn't* she met him? She had met everyone else involved. And what was Malcolm saying about liver damage?

Also, there was the time she'd caught him relabeling a slide. He'd seemed so nervous about it. It had seemed like an honest mistake at the time, but was it? Could that have anything to do with Louis?

It's probably nothing, she told herself, scanning the files. I'll find out that everything is just the way it's supposed to be.

Part of the reason Ginny was at the hospital so early was that she knew she was falling for Malcolm hard. She didn't want to get hurt, the way she had with Ray. She couldn't go through that again. She had to know everything was on the up-and-up, even if it meant spying.

She desperately hoped Malcolm didn't decide to come in early. If he caught her, it would be all over between them. Not to mention the fact that she'd lose her job, too.

Come on, she told herself. It was just one weird-sounding conversation. You can't judge someone by something you overheard—it's not fair. Of course, spying wasn't exactly fair, either,

Ginny thought as she started flipping through the files in the top drawer. Each file folder was numbered and represented a specific patient. She checked the first couple of files, with records for patients she hadn't seen before. Pretty routine stuff, she thought.

Then she saw the folder that Malcolm had been working on a few days earlier—Patient 117848. That was one she wanted to check out. It was the same file he'd been looking for on her first day, and the same slide he'd been fixing the label on. The patient had been part of the two-year trial, and when Ginny had last examined his test results, Malcolm had explained to her that he was suffering from liver damage—but it wasn't related to Alpha II, since he was taking the placebo.

Ginny opened the file and skimmed the patient's results. "Wait a second," she gasped. Patient 117848 *was* taking the drug. It said so in all of his records! So why had Malcolm said that he wasn't?

She grabbed the next few files and looked at the results. More patients with liver damage. But Malcolm hadn't even mentioned to Ginny that liver damage was showing up as a side effect. She'd seen the final report he was working on, he'd showed it to her. He was so proud of how great it had come out. But had it?

Why would Malcolm want to change the results? Unless Alpha II wasn't as effective as he said. Did it actually harm patients more than it helped them? And wasn't Louis supposed to be watching over all of this, making sure everything was being done properly?

"Ginny! What are you doing here?"

Ginny looked up. Malcolm was standing at the door to the lab!

CHAPTER 9

Nancy's muscles tensed as she walked into the Cave and saw Bess already at a table with George. She might not have gone if she'd known Bess would be there.

Bess looked up at her as she approached the table. From the expression on her face, it was clear she wasn't thrilled to see Nancy, either.

"Did you have to kiss Terry like that last night?" she demanded as soon as Nancy slid into a seat across the table. "Right in front of Ned? What were you thinking?"

"Well, good morning to you, too," Nancy replied, raising one eyebrow.

"You really upset him, you know?" Bess went on.

"Well, it's a good thing you were there to console him then, isn't it?" Nancy retorted.

"What's that supposed to mean?" Bess asked.

"I saw you and Ned dancing," Nancy said. "If anyone was out of line, it was you."

"Why? Because I was having a good time? With a friend?" Bess said.

"You guys," George said quietly. "I'm the one who asked you to come here!"

"Fine," Bess said. "But I'm way too upset to eat."

"Do you think *I'm* happy about this?" Nancy said.

"Please, Nancy, Bess, would you listen to me. I might be pregnant!" George announced in a hoarse whisper. Then she burst into tears.

Nancy practically fell out of her chair. "What?"

Bess shot a concerned glance across the table at Nancy. "She said she might be pregnant. Is that true?"

George nodded as Nancy handed her a paper napkin from the dispenser on the table. Tears were rolling down George's cheeks. "Yeah." She sniffled. "My period's late, I've been sick to my stomach—"

"That could be anything," Nancy said reassuringly. "You could have the flu or—"

"Or food poisoning," Bess added helpfully.

"Right!" Nancy said.

George shook her head. "No, it's not just the nausea. I've been having mood swings, and I'm extra tired—"

"That's college," Bess said. "Hey, I feel like that sometimes—"

"It's not just that!" George said. "You guys, my period hasn't been late in five years. This is serious!"

Nancy bit her lip and looked at Bess. She didn't know what they could do to help, but they had to do something. "Okay, so you think you're pregnant," Nancy said slowly. "The first thing we need to do is get one of those tests at the drugstore."

George looked up at her, a pained expression on her face. "I tried that already. It didn't work."

"What do you mean, it didn't work?" Bess asked.

"The results were inconclusive," George said with a groan.

"So, it's simple," Nancy said, putting her hand on George's arm. "We'll just get you another test."

"We'll get you a dozen of them," Bess declared.

George nodded. "Thanks, you guys."

"Why didn't you call us earlier, George?" Bess asked as they stood up.

"I don't know. I was so scared, I didn't want to tell anyone," George said.

"I can't believe you," Bess commented. "Stoic George, trying to handle everything on her own—"

"Wait a second, you mean you haven't even told Will?" Nancy asked, interrupting Bess.

"Not yet," George said. "I wanted to find out for sure first. It might be a false alarm."

Nancy nodded. "We'll know in a couple of hours. Then you can call him when you're ready. Okay?"

George smiled uneasily. "I guess."

"So, do you miss being at the store?" Stephanie asked, stretching her arms over her head. "Because if you really want to get back in time for Berrigan's opening, we could leave now. Right now. Just pack up all our stuff and—"

Jonathan stood behind Stephanie on the private deck outside their room at an old farmhouse that had been converted into a bed and breakfast. He put his hand over her mouth. "I'm not going anywhere."

"You're not?" Stephanie turned around, putting her hands on Jonathan's shoulders.

Jonathan shook his head. "If this is what being kidnapped is like . . . then I don't want to be rescued. At least not until tomorrow."

"I'll alert the authorities," Stephanie promised him.

"Maybe you could tell me something, though."

Jonathan stood back, tapping his chin with his index finger. "What sort of ransom is involved here? I mean, are you going to get money for me, or—"

"Oh, no. This is strictly a . . . charity kidnapping," Stephanie told him. "Free of charge. Although if you really wanted to help, you could try to pay off your captor with kisses."

Jonathan held her by the waist, pulled her close, and kissed her. "How's that?"

"If you want to get back alive, you'll have to do a little better," Stephanie said.

Jonathan picked her up and carried her back into their room.

"Malcolm, uh, hi." Ginny stood up and started shuffling through the papers on his desk. She'd hastily shoved the drawer closed when Malcolm came into the lab.

"What are you doing?" Malcom asked.

"Oh, well, this is really silly. I came in to see you. But you weren't here, so I was studying." Ginny quickly slipped the files she hadn't had time to put back under her notebook, then slid the whole pile into her backpack. "So, how are you?"

"Great," Malcolm said slowly, looking around the lab. "I thought I'd get an early start today, then finish early. Maybe we'll have time to go out to dinner." He came over to Ginny and put his arms around her waist, then looked down at the file cabinet, still opened a crack. "We should really make a night of it tonight."

Ginny stepped out of his grasp. "Malcolm?"

"What?" He reached out and ran his hand down her cheek.

"I have to ask you something," Ginny said.

"Okay," Malcom said, hopping up onto the desk and smiling at her. "Go ahead."

Ginny bit her lip. "It's about your research."

"Our research, you mean," Malcolm corrected her.

Ginny nodded. "Uh, have you been, uh, editing the Alpha Two test results?"

Malcolm frowned. "Editing? What do you mean?"

"Leaving out information," Ginny said.

"What?" Malcolm laughed. "Ginny, you're imagining things."

"No, I'm not. I looked at the files," Ginny said. "And I saw you change the slide labels. I don't think you're putting the correct results into your report."

"Maybe you just didn't understand what you were looking at," Malcolm said in a condescending voice. "Ginny, you've been working in here—what, a week? And you're in your first year of *pre*med?" He shook his head. "How could you possibly think you know what's going on here?"

"I understand the project. You explained it to

me, remember? And I saw you change the results to make it look like Alpha Two helped everyone. In fact, all the people taking the placebo were fine, but the patients taking Alpha Two are suffering from liver damage. I read the files, Malcolm," Ginny said.

"Let me get this straight." Malcolm hopped off the desk and sidled up to Ginny. "You went through my files. You opened a *locked* cabinet, without my permission, because you thought I was trying to doctor my results?" He yanked the file cabinet open, demonstrating that it was unlocked. "Ginny, get real. You've been watching too many hospital dramas on TV." He ran a hand through his hair. "Do yourself a favor and leave the research to me." He shoved the file drawer closed and locked it again, using a key on his key chain.

"So then, everything's under control?" Ginny said, staring at him. "That's what you told Louis, right?"

"What—you're an eavesdropper, too?" Malcolm said. He shook his head. "I thought you were a professional. I thought we were a team. But if you want to creep around drawing false conclusions about confidential information, listening to my phone conversations . . ."

"I couldn't help but overhear," Ginny said. "You told me to meet you here that night."

"Maybe I did. But, Ginny, that's because I

thought I could trust you. But apparently you're not ready for the kind of responsibility a project like this requires," Malcolm said. "So maybe you should just take off today. Come back later and we'll talk about this, try to straighten things out. Your brain's working overtime," Malcolm continued. "You were up too late last night. You're seeing things that don't exist."

"Maybe." Ginny stared at him. She'd seen the files with her own eyes. Did he really think she was that naive? "Okay, I'll go. But I'll be back."

"Fine. See you later," Malcolm said, turning toward the counter. "I have to get to work."

Ginny picked up her backpack, conscious of the patient files inside. She couldn't leave the hospital with them—that would be illegal—and she especially didn't want Malcolm to know which ones she'd checked out. She crouched down and unzipped the outside pocket. To cover taking the files out she stuffed her hat in the pocket. Then she shoved the files under a stack of books, hoping to come back later that day to check them out more carefully.

"Good thing you brought your credit card," George told Bess as they dumped the plastic bag onto George's bed. Five different pregnancy tests spilled out onto the quilt.

Nancy sat down on the bed beside the pile of

boxes. She sifted through them, reading the back of each one.

Bess straddled Pam's desk chair and hung her arms over the top.

George stared at the boxes for a few seconds. She felt a pang in her lower abdomen and winced. "I guess it's time."

Bess and Nancy nodded.

George groaned, as a single tear trailed down her cheek.

"Don't cry!" Nancy said. She jumped off the bed and gave George a hug.

"Yeah," Bess said, standing up and wrapping her arms around her two friends. "Go on, George. We'll wait right here."

George picked out one of the boxes. "You guys are the best, you know that, don't you?" she asked, pausing halfway to the door.

"Yeah, yeah, we know," Bess said. "Now, do I have to escort you to the bathroom or what?"

After George left the room, Bess spun around in Pam's desk chair a few times. Then she looked over at Nancy. She couldn't stand fighting with her, especially when they both needed to be there for George.

"Look, Nancy, I'm sorry I bit your head off at breakfast," she began.

"No, I'm sorry," Nancy said, interrupting her. "I acted like a real jerk."

"You were probably only responding to me. And I didn't mean to sound so angry. But Ned *was* upset," Bess said. "And you did kind of throw Terry in his face."

"Yeah, I know," Nancy admitted.

"You know?" Bess asked, wheeling around on the chair. "Then why did you do it?"

Nancy sighed. "It's hard to explain. I just went a little nuts when I came into the Underground and saw you guys dancing together."

"But you and Ned aren't seeing each other anymore," Bess said. "Anyway, I'm not interested in him that way. But it doesn't make sense for you to still think of him as yours."

Nancy sighed. "I know. It's just that it really hurt my feelings that you or Ned didn't call me when he got here. I thought we were all going out Friday night. Then Stephanie came back to the dorm and told me you and Ned were at the Underground, so I called Terry."

"Why?" Bess asked.

"I don't know. I was just feeling so confused. When I broke up with Jake, I started thinking about how great things had been with Ned," Nancy said. "Then I saw him with you, and you were having such a good time. It made me jealous."

"We weren't trying to make you feel jealous," Bess said. "We're just friends, Nancy. You know that."

Nancy frowned. "Then how come you didn't ask me to come out with you?"

"You know how much he's been helping me deal with Paul's death," Bess began. "We talked most of the night, that's all. It wasn't about you—we didn't ask George or Brian or anyone else to come along, either."

All of a sudden, George burst through the doorway, with a huge smile on her face. "No more tests!" she cried happily.

"Well, it took you long enough," Bess asked. "What happened?"

"I didn't have to take the test. I got my period!" George announced, jumping up and down.

"That's great!" Bess cried, leaping out of the chair. All the tension left her body. She hadn't realized she'd been so worried.

"Phew," Nancy said, wiping her brow. "That makes life a lot easier."

"I never thought I'd be so happy to get it," George said. "So, you guys don't have to stick around. I'm sure you have better things to do on a Saturday."

"Actually, I should be getting back. Ned's waiting for me," Bess said. She glanced uneasily at Nancy.

Maybe I *am* starting to think of him that way. Bess had to admit that she'd always found him very attractive. But she'd never go out with her best friend's old boyfriend, would she?

CHAPTER 10

Ginny walked through the front doors of Weston General Saturday afternoon and got into the elevator. She was determined to talk to Malcolm again. The more she thought about what he'd said earlier, the less sense it made. She wanted him to admit what he was doing and tell her why.

Ginny stepped out of the elevator and nearly bumped right into Hazel Mosely.

"Hi, Dr. Mosely."

"Ginny, what are you doing here on a Saturday?" Dr. Mosely asked.

"I—I came to see Malcolm," Ginny answered. "We have something to talk about."

"Well, I'm glad you're here, Ginny. I have a problem I need to discuss with you."

"Me?" Ginny asked.

"Yes, could you come down to my office please?"

Ginny followed her.

"Sit down," Dr. Mosely directed.

Ginny perched uncomfortably on the edge of a plastic chair. What could this be about? "Have I . . . have I done something wrong?" she asked.

"Yes, you have," Dr. Mosely said. "I've received a complaint about you from Dr. Hendrix."

"What kind of complaint?" Ginny blurted.

"He claimed you made unwanted advances toward him," Dr. Mosely said. "Sexual advances. That's against hospital policy."

"But . . . but he's the one who asked *me* out," Ginny protested.

"A little crush is one thing, Ginny, but propositioning the doctor you're working for, after he's made it clear he's not interested . . ."

"That's not what happened!" Ginny said.

"Oh, no? Then maybe you can explain to me what you're doing here on a Saturday when you're not even scheduled to work."

"We had a, uh, a misunderstanding earlier," Ginny explained. "I wanted to clear it up so it wouldn't interfere with our work."

"According to Dr. Hendrix, it's already affected your work," Dr. Mosely said.

Ginny gripped the edge of her chair. Why was Malcolm doing this to her? She must be onto something. That must have been why Malcolm wanted to get rid of her. And the easiest way for him to do that was to accuse her of something. Something she *hadn't* done. "So, what's going to happen to me?" Ginny asked.

"Well, you'll be suspended temporarily," Dr. Mosely said. "While we look into the charge."

"Temporarily? For how long?" Ginny asked.

"I'm not sure yet. If we find there's no truth to the charge, we'll transfer you to another department, if we can find you a spot."

"Are you saying I'll be kicked out of the hospital?" Ginny asked.

"We won't kick you out, Ginny. Not if we find you innocent," Dr. Mosely said.

Ginny stood up. There was no use arguing with Dr. Mosely. She flung open the door and walked purposefully down the hall. Malcolm had destroyed her career at Weston General before it even began!

"Thanks for meeting me here," Nancy said, pushing her knapsack out of the way so Terry could sit beside her at Java Joe's.

"No problem," Terry replied. "I was ready for a study break." He took a bite of an onion bagel with cream cheese.

"More statistics?" Nancy asked. Terry nodded. "Remind me never to take that class."

"You could always use my incredibly helpful notes," Terry offered.

"Right." Nancy slowly stirred sugar into her cafe latte. "Look, Terry, this is really hard to say, and I hope you won't take it the wrong way."

She hated having to do this. But she'd gotten herself into this mess by kissing Terry, and now she had to get herself out. After talking with Bess earlier, she'd realized what a mistake she'd made.

"I'm sorry about last night," she began awkwardly.

"Sorry? Why?"

"Well, it didn't go exactly as it should have," Nancy said.

"Didn't you have fun?" Terry asked.

"I did. I had a great time," Nancy said. "But I don't know what I was doing last night. I mean, I shouldn't have kissed you. I think I moved too fast. I'm not ready to go out with you, Terry. I'm not ready to go out with anyone," Nancy confessed. "And it was really dumb of me to ask you out when I wasn't sure."

Terry looked down at the table, scratching at a mark in the wood. "So you don't want to see me. Even though we always have a great time together, and even though you said you did want to go out with me last night, which was not even twenty-four hours ago."

Nancy rubbed her forehead, closing her eyes. "I know. I'm sorry, Terry. I was confused. So I made a decision that I wasn't ready for. I do have a great time with you, Terry. I just can't make any kind of commitment to you. And that's not fair."

"So now what?" Terry asked. "Do we go back to being friends?"

"Terry, I know it sounds clichéd," Nancy said, "but that's what I'd like to do."

"Well, I don't know if I can handle that," Terry said. "I'll see you, Nancy." He stood up and walked out of Java Joe's.

Nancy slumped forward in her chair, resting her head on her hands. Couldn't she do anything right?

Will bounced the basketball three times, the same way he always did before every free throw. Concentrate, he told himself. Then he bent his knees and arched the ball toward the basket.

It bounced off the rim with a loud clang.

"That's the twentieth free throw in a row you've missed," Andy commented, grabbing the ball. "I'm killing you. I've hit fourteen, and you've hit zero."

"I know," Will said with a sigh.

"Here, take my turn," Andy offered, tossing the ball to him.

"It won't help," Will said, throwing it back. "I can't concentrate."

"George?" Andy asked.

"George," Will said. "I haven't seen her since the night she told me she wanted some space.

She said she'd call me. She hasn't called, and I'm starting to think she's not going to."

"Come on, man. George loves you," Andy said. "She's probably going through a hard time with school and all, but that doesn't mean she doesn't want to see you."

"Oh, yeah? Then what does it mean? If she's not seeing me?" Will asked.

Andy shrugged. "I don't know."

"Well, think. I mean, why would she need so much space?" Will asked.

Andy walked around the basketball court, dribbling the ball. "I guess if Reva said something like that to me, I'd probably think she was seeing someone else."

"Yeah, that's all I can think, too," Will admitted. And it was making him feel horrible. He wished George would just tell him instead of ignoring him, the way she had been. Didn't she care about him anymore? Weren't they still in love?

"Only one way to find out, dude," Andy said. "Ask her." He tossed the ball hard, straight at Will's chest.

Will reached for the ball, but it bounced off his hands. "Yeah. You're right."

Ginny strode into Java Joe's Saturday afternoon. She'd walked there straight from the hospital, still not knowing what she was going to do.

131

She did know she was too wound up to go back to her room.

She grabbed a cup of decaf coffee and a fudge brownie and paid for them at the cashier's. When she turned around, she noticed Nancy sitting by herself in a corner. Ginny walked over to her, bursting to tell someone what was going on.

"Nancy, you're not going to believe what just happened," Ginny said, sliding into a chair across from Nancy. "Sexual harassment! Me!"

"What—you were harassed? Where—at work? At the hospital, you mean?" Nancy asked, sitting forward. "That's terrible!"

"No." Ginny shook her head vigorously. "I mean, it's terrible, but it's not what you're thinking. I wasn't harassed. I was let go because someone accused *me* of harassing *him.*"

"What? Who would do that?" Nancy asked.

"Malcolm—Dr. Hendrix, I mean," Ginny said, practically spitting his name. "As if he even deserves to be a doctor." Just thinking about what Malcolm had done made Ginny so furious, she couldn't sit still. "Oh, it's not fair to bother you with my problems—I'll talk to you later." She stood up abruptly, knocking over an empty coffee cup with her arm.

"Wait—explain!" Nancy said, grabbing Ginny's sleeve. "You can't leave now!"

Ginny sighed. "Are you sure you want to hear the whole story?"

"Sure, I'm sure," Nancy said. "Maybe I can help. You shouldn't lose your job because some creep accuses you of harassment."

"Well, it's already happened," Ginny told her. She sat back down and unwrapped the plastic from her brownie. "Dr. Mosely told me today not to come back because Malcolm had complained about me."

"Why would he accuse you like that?" Nancy asked. "Didn't you guys go out last night?"

"Yeah. And everything was fine, until I started asking him questions about the work he's been doing," Ginny explained. "He didn't like my questions so he decided to get me fired. Since he's the doctor, and I'm only a volunteer, I'm expendable. Now he can go back to changing his dumb test results and switching slides around—"

"Hold on," Nancy said. "What are you talking about? Was he changing the results of his research?"

"I'm not a hundred percent sure, but I'm pretty positive because of what I ran across in the files. I think he's been changing the results so that the drug he's studying looks better than it is," Ginny said.

"Why would he do that?" Nancy asked. "Wouldn't that be harmful to patients?"

"It could be," Ginny said. "But apparently he doesn't care. He probably thinks he'll be in some hotshot job before anyone figures it out."

"But once it is discovered that the drug doesn't work, the faulty results will be traced back to him, won't they?" Nancy asked.

"Not for a while, and not if he keeps firing everyone who catches on," Ginny said. "A doctor might think that his patient is the only one who ever got sick from the medicine without the proper test results."

"Well, I'm sure there's some way we can put a stop to this," Nancy said. "We just have to figure out how."

"We? You mean you'll help me?" Ginny asked.

"Sure. I've been looking for an idea for a newspaper article," Nancy told her, standing up. "And this seems to be perfect for an exposé on faked research results at Weston General."

"An exposé?" Ginny said. She wasn't sure she wanted to do anything that drastic to Malcolm. "But what if I'm wrong?" she asked Nancy.

"Don't worry. I won't publish anything until we confirm the facts," Nancy assured her.

"George? We need to talk," Will announced. He marched past George into her room without waiting for an invitation.

"Will, I was just about to call you," George said, flustered.

"Oh, sure. I bet," Will said. He peered around the room, trying to find some evidence that another guy had been there. He didn't see anything out of the ordinary, but that didn't mean that nothing had been going on.

"I was!" George protested. "I wanted to know what you were up to this weekend and—"

"George, sit down," Will said, pacing around the room.

"Why?" George asked.

"I've got something to say to you," Will said. "I've tried really hard to give you your space and be understanding, but I can't take this cold shoulder routine, George, I really can't. You can quit trying to hide the truth from me. I *know* what's going on."

George edged toward her desk. Her face turned slightly pale. "You—you do?" she stammered.

"Yes. It's so obvious, I don't know why it didn't occur to me right off the bat, but it didn't." Will shook his head. "I was stupid, that's why."

"Will, I—"

Will held up his hand. "No, George, let me finish." He took a deep breath to try to calm down. "You've fallen in love with someone else, haven't you?"

He paused, glancing at George. She looked shocked, as if she couldn't believe he'd found out the truth. So it was true.

"I guess I can't change your mind. But could you at least stop treating me like I'm some . . .

kid who doesn't deserve to know any better?" Will continued. "Just tell me the truth, George. Are you dating another guy? If you are, then I wish you'd just break up with me instead of sneaking around behind my back."

"Break up with you?" George's voice quivered. "No, Will, no!" She burst into tears and threw herself into his arms.

He held her close as she hugged him. Will had never seen her cry like that, and he felt more confused than ever.

CHAPTER 11

"Are you sure they'll let us use it?" Nancy asked as she followed Ginny down the hall at Weston General to the nearest copier.

Ginny nodded. "I didn't turn in my ID." She fished the small plastic card out of her pocket and clipped it to her green volunteer lab coat. "I'm sure none of the nurses on the floor know that I've been suspended—we don't work together that much. The only one I really know likes me."

"Okay, just copy those patient files as fast as you can," Nancy said. She wandered around the hallway, looking at various announcements posted on the bulletin board.

"Working late tonight, Ginny?" one of the nurses asked.

137

"I'm almost done, Erica," she said, shoving the documents into the sheet feeder. "Just need to make a few copies first."

When she was done, Ginny handed the copies to Nancy to stuff into her knapsack. Then they hurried back to the lab where Ginny returned the original files to Malcolm's filing cabinet.

"Okay, they're back, safe and sound," Ginny said, slipping out of her lab coat and putting it back on the chair she used to sit in. "Now all we have to do is get out of here—"

"Shh," Nancy said. "Someone's coming!" She heard footsteps moving down the hall toward the lab. They stopped right outside the lab.

"Don't worry—I've got plans tonight!" a voice called out.

"It's Malcolm!" Ginny said, grabbing Nancy's elbow.

"What should we do?" Nancy whispered.

"I've just got to make one call and then I'll be out of here," Malcolm said.

"Come on—we can hide down here!" Ginny pulled Nancy down underneath the assistant's desk.

Nancy wrapped her arms around her knees and squatted beside Ginny. She was a lot taller than Ginny, so it was hard to fit her long legs in the small space. Let's hope it's a short phone call, she thought.

Nancy heard footsteps coming their way. She

concentrated on breathing as quietly as possible. She didn't want to think about what would happen if Malcolm found them. Was it against the law to be in a hospital lab without authorization? Probably.

A chair scraped against the linoleum floor as Nancy heard Malcolm pick up a telephone. He sounded as if he were across the room at another desk.

"Louis? Hi, it's Malcolm. Yeah. Yeah, I said I'd get back to you and I am. Uh-huh. Yeah. Actually, I think I might have found some more investors."

Nancy looked at Ginny and raised an eyebrow. Ginny had told her about the other phone call Malcolm had made to Louis and how he'd said Louis was a medical monitor. Why would a medical monitor want to know about investors? Nancy wondered.

"Nothing for sure yet. I'll be meeting with a couple of them next week. I'm sure once they hear the deal, they'll be interested. Anyway, I'd better run. Yeah. We'll talk more on Monday. Okay." Malcolm hung up the phone.

Nancy crossed her fingers, hoping he would leave right away. Her knees were starting to shake. She could hear him looking through some papers on his desk. Then he got up and started wandering around the lab. There was a loud whir, and Nancy heard the sound of a paper shredder chewing up documents.

Ginny's fists were clenched, and she looked as if she was ready to burst out from under the desk and punch Malcolm. "I bet he's getting rid of the test results," she whispered frantically.

"It's okay," Nancy mouthed, touching Ginny's hand lightly. "We've got copies, remember?"

A few moments later the door to the lab opened and closed. They waited another minute to make sure Malcolm had left. Then Nancy crept out from under the desk and peeked over the top of it. The lab was empty.

"Come on," she whispered to Ginny. "Let's go. And, please, tell me you know about some back stairwell."

"It's this way," Ginny said as they hurried out of the lab, and down the hall, away from the nurses' station and elevator.

Nancy took the steps two at a time with Ginny right behind her. "Wait a second—shouldn't we take the stuff out of the shredder?" Ginny asked, following Nancy down the stairs. "Maybe it'd help."

"No, you can't make sense of whatever's been destroyed—trust me," Nancy said, glancing over her shoulder. "I shredded something by mistake in my dad's office once. A major piece of evidence for a case he was working on. I think he wanted to shred me."

They finally burst out of the stairwell and into the parking lot. Nancy felt her heart start beating even faster as adrenaline rushed through her.

"That was too close," Ginny panted, leaning against the wall to take a breath.

"Definitely," Nancy said. "Hey, what do you think he meant by investors?"

"I have no idea," Ginny said, shaking her head. "He told me Louis was a medical monitor—you know, someone who oversees the whole drug-trial process to keep an eye on the company."

"So why would a medical monitor care about investors?" Nancy asked.

"Well, sometimes the monitors work for the actual drug companies," Ginny explained.

"Yeah, okay. But Malcolm doesn't work for the drug company. He works for the hospital," Nancy reasoned.

"True." Ginny nodded.

"Did he ever say anything that made you think he was—I don't know—involved in something besides research at the hospital?" Nancy asked.

"Well . . ." Ginny thought for a minute. "When we went out to dinner at Les Peches, he did mention something about how there were ways to make money when you were in med school so you didn't go hopelessly into debt."

"What did he say exactly?" Nancy asked as they headed back toward the Wilder campus.

"He was really vague, actually," Ginny said. "I kind of made a joke out of it. He said you had to play your cards right, and I asked if he meant going to Vegas. He laughed and then changed the subject." She shrugged. "Why? What do you think he meant?"

"I'm not sure," Nancy said. "Come on. Let's go back to the suite and see what we can figure out."

"Some Saturday night, huh?" Ginny asked, wrinkling her nose.

"Believe me, Ginny. After the week I've had, I can't think of a better way to spend it," Nancy admitted. At least this way, she knew what she was doing. She'd really hurt Terry—and Ned—and she wasn't ready to forgive herself for that.

George snuggled closer to Will. Tears dripped off her face onto his sweatshirt.

"George, come on. Stop crying." Will put his hand on the back of her head. "It makes me feel even worse. And besides, you're getting me soaked."

George stepped away and looked up at him, her eyes brimming with tears. "Will, I'm not seeing anyone else! How could you think that of me?"

"Gee, I don't know." Will stared at her. "Could it be that you've avoided me for the past several days?"

"I know I have, Will. And I'm sorry," George said. She grabbed a tissue from the box on her dresser and wiped away her tears. "But . . ." She took a deep breath. "The thing is . . . until a few hours ago, I thought I was pregnant."

"What?" Will's eyes opened wide.

"Yeah. That's what I thought you'd say." George laughed lightly.

"No, really. What are you talking about?" Will asked, putting a hand on her shoulder. "You thought you were pregnant. So you decided not to tell me? Excuse me, but wouldn't I be at least halfway responsible?"

"Well . . . yeah, but—"

"Well, yeah, nothing," Will scoffed. "Why didn't you tell me?"

"I don't know," George said with a shrug. "I guess I didn't want to worry you. And I thought, I shouldn't tell you until I knew for sure."

"Why not worry me, too?" Will asked. "Or are you into this martyr thing?"

"No, it's not that. I guess I was afraid," George confessed.

"Afraid of what? Being pregnant?"

"That, and that you'd leave me or something," George said.

"Me, leave you. Because you got pregnant? George, I love you. I'd love you whether you were pregnant or not. But I *don't* love being kept in the dark. That's not fair."

George nodded. "I know. I guess I was just so wrapped up in worrying about myself that I forgot about you. I mean, I didn't *forget* about you, of course. But I didn't stop to think that you'd feel bad about being left out."

"Oh, yeah." Will looked up at the ceiling, rolling his eyes. "Getting blown off always makes me feel all warm and tingly inside. George, if you'd leveled with me, we both would have felt better. You see that, don't you?"

"I'll be honest with you from now on," George promised. "About everything."

"Good." Will put his hands on George's waist and pulled her close for a kiss.

For a moment George lost herself in his embrace. She'd missed being close to Will and she loved how she felt when she was with him. But something was different now. She couldn't quite enjoy it the way she had before. She stepped back, separating herself from Will. "If I'm going to be honest about everything, I have to say something."

"Okay." Will brushed her forehead with his lips. "Go ahead."

"After what just happened, and the week I went through . . . well, I'm not sure if we should be so close anymore. I mean, I'm not ready for the possible consequences. And until I am, it's not fair to me, or you, or anyone else—for me to keep sleeping with you," George said.

Will's face fell. "You're kidding."

"It's too scary," George argued. She looked anxiously at Will. Maybe saying this was taking a bigger risk than saying she thought she was pregnant, but she couldn't let herself give in to what Will wanted. They both had to be comfortable about having an intimate relationship or it wasn't worth having one.

"Well, if you feel that way, okay." Will shrugged. "We'll take it slow for a while."

"Thanks." George breathed a sigh of relief. "You realize you're the best boyfriend in the whole world, don't you?"

"Well, yeah, I kind of thought so," Will said, swaggering a bit.

George stood on her tiptoes and kissed him on the cheek. "You're so modest." She'd never loved Will more than she did at that moment.

"Do you want to dance?"

Ned shook his head.

"Come on," Bess urged. "Last night you wouldn't let me take a break." She watched Ned for a minute. Since they'd arrived at Club Z, Ned had been off in another world—one without loud music! They were sitting on the stairs to one of the upper levels of the space, which had been transformed from an old warehouse into the hottest club around.

Bess looked down at the dance floor at her

Kappa friends all dancing and laughing. They were having a wild time.

Ned seemed oblivious to the whole scene. He just kept looking at Bess. It was starting to make her feel a little uncomfortable.

"Ned? Are you sure you don't want to dance?" she asked.

"No. I'd rather just sit here with you," Ned said.

Bess toyed with one of her shoelaces. "Feeling lazy, huh?" she joked.

"No." Ned laughed. "It's not that." He paused for a minute. "Bess, can I say something?"

"What—you don't like this song? You're waiting for the next one, right?" Bess teased.

"No. Actually, I was sitting here thinking about how I don't want to go back to Emerson tomorrow."

Bess's eyes widened as Ned reached for her hand.

"We've had such a great time together this weekend. I don't want to leave."

Bess's heart started beating faster. "Well, I . . . I don't want you to go, either," she confessed.

"You don't?" Ned asked.

Bess shook her head. "Maybe I shouldn't tell you this, but I've been thinking of you differently, Ned. I mean, as more than just a friend." She felt light-headed, as if she was about to faint from nervousness. What was she doing, telling Ned about her feelings for him? What if he didn't like her, that way?

"I know," Ned said. "I mean—I've been feeling differently about you, too. Like . . . I've never thought of you before. You're so pretty, Bess—I must have been blind not to have noticed. And spending time with you is so easy, as if we're always on the same wavelength."

Bess stared into Ned's eyes and felt as though she was about to do something very, very foolish. She wanted to kiss him.

Me and Ned? No. That can't happen! It was just as Victoria had said—she was only turning to Ned because she missed Paul. And she couldn't replace Paul with anyone—no matter how much she loved Ned. As a friend, she reminded herself.

"Ned, I-I'm sorry," Bess said. "I can't do this right now. I mean, I do have feelings for you. But I'm afraid that they're not quite real. I think maybe I'm turning to you because I lost Paul. And I don't want to use you that way. Our friendship's too important."

"No—I'm the one who should be sorry. I shouldn't have said anything," Ned apologized. "I know what a hard time you've had, and that you're probably sort of vulnerable. You're one of my best friends, and I don't want that to change."

"So." Bess looked around the dance floor uneasily. "That's the end of that."

"Right," Ned said, nodding.

"Right," Bess said. She glanced at Ned out of the corner of her eye. They could say it was the end, but that didn't change her feelings for him. She was attracted to him—she couldn't deny that even to herself.

"For now," Ned added, suddenly leaning over and kissing Bess on the cheek. "Who knows about the future?"

CHAPTER 12

Ginny peered over Nancy's shoulder at the computer screen. They'd been surfing the Web on Reva Ross's computer for the past half hour. Nancy was busy searching for more data on Revolution Drugs, the company that had developed Alpha II.

"Do you really think we'll find anything about Malcolm?" Ginny asked.

"Anything we find out about the company should help," Nancy said, tapping into the Revolution Drugs home page on the Web.

Ginny stared at the promotional information. "That isn't going to tell us much. It's basically one big ad."

"No, but there's a section called 'Who's Who—' maybe that has something," Nancy said.

As Nancy fiddled with the mouse, clicking onto different screens, Ginny thought about the first time she'd met Malcolm. He'd immediately made an effort to include her, referring to her as a colleague. Then he'd taken her to dinner, and they'd shared those romantic kisses. She'd thought he was the guy who was going to make her forget all about Ray. He was so interesting, and so smart, but he'd been lying to her all along.

Am I really that bad a judge of character? she wondered.

"Hey, Ginny, what was the name of that guy again? The one Malcolm called?" Nancy asked.

"Louis," Ginny said. "The medical monitor."

Nancy pointed to the computer screen. "See this? The owner of Revolution Drugs is named Louis Wilson."

"The owner? Do you think it could be a coincidence?" Ginny asked.

"It could be," Nancy agreed. "But Malcolm was telling Louis about investors yesterday. And you heard him tell Louis he'd take care of the results. If it was this Louis, then Malcolm could be working directly for the owner."

"And the test results for Alpha Two would be rigged to come out in favor of Revolution Drugs," Ginny concluded. "But why would Malcolm care? Unless . . ."

"Unless someone was paying him to care," Nancy suggested.

"Which would mean he could buy his Porsche and pay off all his student loans," Ginny said. "Whether or not the drug works."

"I have an idea," Nancy said, gazing at the computer screen. "If Louis isn't really the medical monitor of this project, who is? There would have to be one—or more than one, right?" she asked Ginny.

"Malcolm told me it's standard procedure," Ginny said, "but I never saw one in the lab. He could have been lying."

"True, he could have been," Nancy said. "But drug tests usually do have to be monitored." She tapped at the computer keys, searching for more information. "Keyword: Alpha II," she typed.

A screen with the drug's logo popped up in front of them. "An exciting new drug now being prepared for the market," an ad proclaimed in big letters.

"Look!" Nancy pointed at the bottom of the screen. "Test run by Dr. Thomas Willard, assisted by Dr. Malcolm Hendrix, monitored by Dr. Susan Lanter, Dr. Jennifer Hardigg, and Dr. Byron Smith!"

"So, Louis isn't the name of one of the medical monitors," Ginny said. "At least, not according to this. It could be outdated."

"True," Nancy agreed.

"But if those are supposed to be the monitors, where are they? Why aren't they at the lab?"

"Well, maybe they don't come in that often. Or maybe they don't even exist," Nancy suggested.

"Oh, come on. They have to exist," Ginny said.

Nancy pushed the mouse around its pad, thinking. "Not necessarily. I mean, if Malcolm's going to change test results to make sure the company profits, I doubt Louis and the rest of his company would stop there. Maybe they'd try to get around having monitors, too."

"But Dr. Willard would never stand for that. Neither would the hospital administration or the FDA or—"

"Okay. So maybe these doctors do exist," Nancy said slowly. "But maybe they're in on this, too. It's possible they just sign off on the test results Malcolm provides to them without checking them over—because that's what they're paid to do. You said that drug companies sometimes hire the monitors, right? So Louis could be paying them to look the other way," Nancy concluded.

"So now what?" Ginny asked.

"We've got to figure out a way to get into this company," Nancy said, standing up. "The headquarters for Revolution Drugs are in Seattle. Any ideas?"

"Take a major road trip?" Ginny joked, trying to smile.

"I wish," Nancy said. "Let's think. Malcolm's

got to be doing all this for something pretty big. I mean, it's a huge risk for a doctor to take. Nobody would do it without the promise of tons of money at the end. He must have a lot invested in the company. In fact, he might even own part of it."

"How could he?" Ginny asked. "With all the debt from his loans? Anyway, his name's not in the computer."

"No, but he could be a silent partner. If he owns part of the company, and the drug gets approved, millions of people will buy it, and he'll make millions of dollars."

Ginny almost felt sick to her stomach. "We can't let that happen, Nancy. This drug is only minimally effective. And it's going to offer all these patients false hope. What can we do?"

Nancy looked out the window for a minute. "Remember how Malcolm said he had some other investors in mind—when he called Louis the other night?"

"Sure," Ginny said.

"I could pretend to be an investor," Nancy offered. "I'll call Louis in Seattle and ask him if there's someone I could meet in the area. If he says Malcolm . . ."

"Do you think you can trick Malcolm into telling you what's going on?" Ginny asked.

"I don't know. But it's worth a shot. Come on.

Let's go to my room and I'll call the company," Nancy said.

"Nancy? It's Sunday," Ginny reminded her. "Businesses are closed."

"Oh. You're right." Nancy's shoulders slumped forward. "Well, I can leave a message, ask Louis Wilson to set up a meeting for me and call me Monday with the details. If they're as anxious to find more investors as they sounded the other night, I'm sure they'll get back to me right away. Don't worry—I'll sound really, really rich. I'll call myself . . . Courtney Howard."

"Courtney Howard . . . Aren't you the one who just inherited an incredibly giant trust fund?" Ginny asked.

"Exactly," Nancy said with a smile. "And after I call there, let's go to the hospital. Maybe we can find out more about the other so-called medical monitors."

"Good idea," Ginny said.

"I hate long goodbyes." Ned stuffed the last of his things into his duffel bag. "Just wave from the window, okay?"

Bess nodded. She, Ned, and Leslie had been reading the Sunday newspaper, eating bagels, and sipping coffee and juice for the past hour. Bess had been dreading this moment.

"We'll see each other soon," Ned promised.

"Thanks for coming," Bess said, trying to sound cheerful.

Ned picked up his duffel bag, said goodbye to Leslie, and walked to the door. He looked at Bess. "Well, I guess this is it."

Bess ran over and threw her arms around Ned, giving him a big hug. "I'll miss you," she said.

"I'll call you," he said, hugging her back.

Bess watched Ned disappear down the hallway. She closed the door and wandered over to the window that looked out on the parking lot. She watched as Ned put his duffel into the trunk of his car, then got behind the steering wheel.

"He's a really nice guy," Leslie commented, sitting down at her desk. "If I were you, I wouldn't watch him drive off. That always makes me really sad."

Bess sighed. "You're right." She left the window and went over to her bed, which needed straightening. She tucked in the sheets and pulled up the comforter. She stacked up some magazines and then got out her organizer to check her homework assignments for the weekend.

She was about to pull out her books when there was a knock at the door. "Come in!" Bess called.

Ned walked into the room. "My car won't start. A guy in the parking lot tried to give me a jump, but the engine is dead." He dropped his duffel bag on the floor.

"So your car's totally out of commission?" Bess asked, trying not to sound excited at the prospect of spending more time with Ned. After all, it was a huge inconvenience for him.

"Sorry," Bess said. She couldn't keep from smiling.

"I don't see their names anywhere," Nancy commented, running her finger down the list of doctors posted at the hospital's main desk. She glanced again at the small sheet of paper in her hand: Lanter, Hardigg, and Smith. None of the doctors' names appeared on the directory. "Maybe they don't exist after all."

"They have to. They probably wouldn't work here, though. I mean, they must be affiliated with another hospital or are in private practice or something," Ginny observed. "To keep everything more objective."

"Maybe," Nancy agreed. "Let's find a phone book and look them up. They've got to be local, if they're checking in from time to time."

"I've got an even better idea," Ginny said. "Let's go upstairs and ask at the nurses' station if anyone's ever heard of them." She and Nancy rushed to the elevator.

A minute later they stepped off on the fourth floor. Ginny walked over to the nurses' station. "Hi, Erica. How's it going?"

"Oh, hi, Ginny." Erica looked up from a chart she was studying.

"This is my friend Nancy, from Wilder," Ginny said. "We came in to check on a couple of things."

"You're not working again, are you? Saturday and Sunday—that's a nurse's schedule, not a volunteer's." She smiled faintly.

Ginny frowned. "No. I'm, uh, not working. But I had to check on something. For . . . for Malcolm."

"Really?" Erica seemed surprised.

"Yeah. Well, see, it's this report I'm doing, for school. A big paper, actually, all about the work I'm doing here. I have to write about the research—you know, to make sure that I get credit hours and all."

"Oh." Erica nodded. "So how can I help you?"

"Well, you know those medical monitors who check on the Alpha Two research, right? I was wondering if you could give me their numbers, so I could interview them for my paper," Ginny said.

"Huh?" Erica looked confused.

"The medical monitors. You know, Louis and Dr. Hardigg, Dr. Lanter, and—"

Erica shook her head. "I don't know who you're talking about, Ginny."

"They're the doctors who monitor the research and make sure it's being done correctly," Nancy told her. "They might work for the drug company."

"I'm not familiar with them—sorry," Erica said. "But you know how busy it gets around here, Ginny. I don't see every single thing that goes on around here. Wait a second—I see Dr. Mosely coming out of her office. I'm sure she knows who they are."

Ginny grabbed Nancy's arm. She had to get out of there before Dr. Mosely saw her, or they'd blow the whole thing! "No—thanks, Erica. I've got to run."

She pulled Nancy around the corner, then down the hall in the opposite direction. "If Dr. Mosely finds out I'm here, she'll tell Malcolm, and we'll never discover the truth," she told Nancy.

"Then let's get out of here. If it turns out that Malcolm owns part of Revolution Drugs, I have a feeling that phony medical monitors are going to be the least of his problems," Nancy said.

"I think we ought to go away every weekend," Jonathan said, unpacking his suitcase. They'd checked out of the bed and breakfast early and driven back in time for Jonathan's afternoon shift at the store. "Unfortunately there's stuff like work . . ."

"Minor detail," Stephanie said with a wave of her hand.

"Not to mention your classes. I'm sure you have a ton of homework to catch up on," Jonathan said.

"Actually, I worked ahead," Stephanie told him. "Since *I* knew we were going away this weekend."

"I love the fact that you surprised me," Jonathan said. "This is the best weekend I've ever had. In fact, it's going to be impossible to go back to the real world."

"So let's not," Stephanie said, taking his hand.

"We have to," Jonathan told her. "But we don't have to forget about this weekend." He leaned over and kissed her neck.

Stephanie sighed. "As long as you keep reminding me like that, I should be able to get through the week."

But she couldn't help wishing she weren't going back to her little dorm room and leaving Jonathan at his apartment. She'd enjoyed being with him all weekend. She didn't want that feeling of closeness to end.

On Sunday evening at six o'clock, Nancy stopped outside Les Peches and checked her reflection in the mirror in her compact. She'd borrowed a sophisticated business suit from Casey and had styled her hair with lots of hair spray. She had much more makeup on than usual. She was wearing the diamond earrings her father had given her for her sixteenth birthday, and she was carrying a leather briefcase.

Louis Wilson had returned her call just minutes after she'd telephoned him. Apparently he was as eager to find new investors as Nancy was to invest. He'd set up a meeting with his co-owner, who "just happened" to live in the area. "Malcolm Hendrix will meet you for drinks at a restaurant called Les Peches at six o'clock," Mr. Wilson had told her when he called back. "Look for a tall man with brown hair."

Nancy opened the door to the restaurant and walked in. A man sitting at a table stood up, signaling to her.

He was even more handsome than Ginny had described. He had on an Italian suit, and his smile was radiant.

"Courtney?" he asked as Nancy approached him.

"Yes," Nancy said. "And you are . . . ?"

"Malcolm Hendrix. It's a pleasure." Malcolm shook her hand. "Please, sit down."

Nancy noticed that he dropped the "doctor" from his name when he introduced himself. "I'm not accustomed to discussing investment opportunities in restaurants," Nancy said in as snobby a tone as she could manage as she slid into a chair, putting her briefcase beside her on the floor. "You *do* have an office, don't you?"

"Oh, of course. But the company's main offices

are in Seattle—as you know, since you talked to Louis earlier today," Malcolm said. "I'm a silent partner. I have business that keeps me here in Weston."

"Really? What kind of business?" Nancy asked. As the waitress took her order for mineral water, she shifted slightly in her seat and brushed her hand against her stomach, making sure the small tape recorder she'd borrowed from the *Wilder Times* office was still in place.

"Medical work," Malcolm said. "Actually, I'm doing my residency at Weston General. That's how I found out about the project. And it's one I'm very excited about," Malcolm said. "If you come on board with us, I'm sure you'll be, too. Now, if you don't mind my asking, how does someone as young as you come to have so much money to invest?"

"I inherited a trust fund from my parents when I turned twenty-one," Nancy said briskly. "But I could ask the same of you. You're awfully young to be the co-owner of a pharmaceutical company. Where did you get your capital?"

"My father's a doctor," Malcolm replied without skipping a beat, "and my mother comes from a well-established New England family. I've been making my own investments for years."

Nancy nodded. It sounded like a stock answer Malcolm had recited for all investors. She wondered if any of it was true. She took a sip from the glass of mineral water the waitress had placed in front of her. "So, what can you tell me about Revolution Drugs?"

"How did you hear about the company?" Malcolm asked, leaning forward.

"An article in the newspaper," Nancy said, "about new developments in medical research."

"Revolution Drugs is on the forefront. Our first major product is a drug called Alpha Two," Malcolm explained. "It's a heart medication. A completely new type. It's used to help patients who've already had mild to moderate heart attacks. With Alpha Two, they won't have another."

"Yes, that's what I understand," Nancy said. "And it's being prepared for the marketplace right now?"

Malcolm nodded. "It's in the final stages of testing."

"And there are no problems with the drug? No major side effects?" Nancy asked.

"Nothing that would prevent the drug from being approved by the FDA," Malcolm said.

"Really," Nancy commented. "That's remarkable. But I thought the article mentioned something about potential liver damage." She looked at Malcolm, trying to see whether her questions were making him nervous. He seemed to be as confident as ever as he shook his head.

"In the beginning, before it was fine-tuned,

perhaps, but not now. Only a very small percentage of patients experience a problem," Malcolm assured her. "And that's true with virtually any medication." He lifted a glass of mineral water to his lips and took a sip.

"So if I were to invest in this company, I could expect a favorable return," Nancy said.

"Definitely," Malcolm said. "Once we bring the drug into the market, I expect it to be prescribed by doctors around the country and eventually around the world. And since you're getting in on the ground floor, so to speak . . . well, your trust fund could easily grow to three or four times its size."

Nancy lifted her eyebrows. "And you expect the FDA to approve Alpha Two—just like that?" She snapped her fingers.

"Well, it's a slow process, of course. But because we've had such great success with the drug so far, we don't anticipate any problems." Malcolm smiled. "So, what do you think? I can give you a prospectus, if you like."

"Yes, that would help," Nancy said. "I'm definitely interested. But I'll have to meet with my financial advisor and see about diverting some money from other areas. Could we get together tomorrow?"

"Of course," Malcolm said eagerly, his dark brown eyes shining with excitement. "Courtney, you won't regret this decision."

"I certainly hope not. There's a lot riding on this." More than you could possibly imagine, she thought, watching Malcolm. He was as confident and charming as Ginny had described him. "Shall I come by the hospital later and find you?"

"No!" Malcolm said loudly. "My office isn't a good place. We can meet at a little café near the hospital. It's called the Broadway Bistro."

"Great" Nancy said. "How's ten o'clock?"

"Now," Malcolm said, "would you like to order dinner?"

Nancy declined, wanting to get out of there. She heaved a sigh of relief as she walked away from Malcolm. She'd pulled off her rich-girl impression, at least for now.

CHAPTER 13

Ginny stood outside Malcolm's apartment door. She tried to convince herself that she should at least be thankful that she'd known Malcolm only a short time and that their relationship hadn't gone far.

That didn't mean it didn't hurt, though. Finding out Malcolm was a lousy person and losing her job weren't exactly what she'd planned when she signed up to volunteer at the hospital.

Ginny wasn't convinced that Nancy was right when she said they had enough evidence to get Malcolm kicked off the hospital staff. She wanted *more* than enough evidence. She pressed the Record button on the microrecorder Nancy had lent her. She was carrying it in the outside pocket of her purse.

She rang the doorbell a few times and stood back. It was early Monday morning and Malcolm should be getting ready to leave for the hospital.

Malcolm opened the door wearing nothing but a towel wrapped around his waist. "Ginny, what are you doing here?" he asked, slicking his hair back.

Ginny forced herself to ignore what a great body Malcolm had. Look away, she told herself, before he charms you all over again. Just concentrate on getting some information out of him. "Hi, Malcolm. Listen. I wanted to apologize for acting like such a brat. I wanted to talk to you about it."

"Well, Ginny, I don't really know what there is to talk about," Malcolm said.

"There's a lot," Ginny said, walking past him into his apartment. "I've been really upset about the way things ended between us." To put it mildly, she thought. But she wouldn't be upset if he managed to let a few facts slip . . . like what he'd really been up to.

"I was just taking a shower—" Malcolm began to protest.

"You can finish it later," Ginny said, pacing around his living room. "Please? I want to know why you accused me of sexual harassment. Why you wanted me out of the hospital. Malcolm, I thought we were in—"

"In love?" Malcolm scoffed, closing the door.

"No. But maybe falling in love," Ginny said in a soft voice.

"Yeah. I did, too," Malcolm said, his face softening.

"So what happened?" Ginny asked.

"Well . . ." Malcolm looked at her, folding his arms across his chest, the softness gone. "Do the words *snooping around* mean anything to you? I caught you looking in my files."

"But I was just trying to help with the research," Ginny argued. "You said we were a team. You invited me to work on everything with you."

"Not everything. And undermining my work isn't exactly what I call helping." Malcolm shook his head.

"How did I undermine your work?" Ginny asked.

"You listened in on phone conversations. You went over my work. You accused me of changing the drug trial results—"

"Well, didn't you?" Ginny asked.

"That's not the point," Malcolm argued.

"But didn't you?" Ginny pressed. "I'm not saying it's wrong, Malcolm. I just want to understand why. It was my project, too. Our project. You said so."

"It was never your project," Malcolm said. "It was mine. Do you think I'm about to share millions of dollars with some freshman volunteer?"

"What?" Ginny pretended to be shocked. "Millions of dollars?"

"I needed those test results to turn out a certain way. When they didn't, I made slight alterations," Malcolm said.

"But what about the medical monitor, Louis? Didn't he catch the mistakes?" Ginny asked.

Malcolm laughed. "Hardly. Louis isn't a medical monitor, which is how much you know. But you had to point out how I edited the results, didn't you? You didn't tell anyone, did you?"

"No, of course not! Malcolm, I really cared about you," Ginny said. "Please, can't you help me get my job back? Tell Dr. Mosely you made up those charges and—"

"Get you back in the lab with me?" Malcolm scoffed. "Ginny, I don't want you anywhere *near* that hospital. Don't you understand? It's too bad you decided to make everything so difficult because I had no choice but to get you fired. You were in the way. But I really hated having to do it. Because I was falling for you. I cared about you. Now, if you don't mind, I need to shower and get dressed. I've got an important meeting later," he announced, heading for his bedroom.

Yes, you do, Ginny thought, heading for the door. And so do I.

"Dr. Willard? May I speak to you for a second?" Ginny paused beside Dr. Willard's table in the cafeteria. He was by himself, for which she was grateful. It would make everything that much easier.

"What about?" Dr. Willard asked, glancing up at her.

"My name is Ginny Yuen. I was working in the research lab, with Dr. Hendrix," Ginny quickly explained.

"Yes, you look familiar," Dr. Willard said. "What is it?"

"I have some information about Alpha Two that I think you need to know," Ginny told him. She glanced nervously at the clock on the wall. She had to get Dr. Willard over to the Broadway Bistro by ten o'clock. "Could you give me a few minutes of your time? It's private, so I'd like to meet in your office."

"Well, I'm not sure why I should," Dr. Willard said. "This is the only free time I've got all day. Besides"—he pushed his glasses up on the bridge of his nose—"aren't you the volunteer who was suspended?"

"Well, yes, but the information I have is related to that," Ginny said. "It's really important, Dr. Willard. I'd never bother you if it weren't."

"Hmm. Well, it can't hurt, I suppose," Dr. Willard grumbled. He pushed his tray away and stood up. "I'll give you five minutes."

Ginny looked at the clock as they walked out

of the cafeteria. Five minutes should just about do it.

"Dr. Willard, it's all here." Ginny spread out the copies of Patient 117848's original test results, and the modified results from another patient's blood test Malcolm had entered on 117848's report. "This patient experienced liver damage on Alpha Two. But his results weren't included in Malcolm's report. Instead, he took the blood workup results from a patient taking the placebo, and entered this data in the file of patient 117848. And this falsifying of the data is just one example of many. Malcolm's report makes it look as if Alpha Two is much safer than it really is."

Dr. Willard studied the papers for several moments, using a pen to track results that hadn't made it onto the final report. "Yes, I see. But I don't understand why Malcolm would do this," Dr. Willard observed.

"He has money invested in Revolution Drugs, the company that manufactures Alpha Two," Ginny explained.

"Invested?" Dr. Willard looked startled.

"Actually, he's one of the owners," Ginny said. "Here, listen to this. A friend of mine pretended to be a potential investor and met with Malcolm. Then I went to see him to ask why he got me fired." She took the microrecorder from her pocket and played back both her and Nancy's conversations with Malcolm.

Dr. Willard sat forward in his chair, listening intently. "This is ridiculous. He can't do this," he muttered under his breath.

Ginny stopped the tape. "I know. And when I confronted him with it, he got rid of me. You heard that part, right?"

Dr. Willard nodded. Then he looked at Ginny as if an idea had suddenly occurred to him. "But how do I know the person on tape is Malcolm? He could be anyone. You could be getting back at Dr. Hendrix for your falling-out. I mean, for all I know, you're the one who completed this faulty report."

Ginny nodded. She'd prepared herself for questions like this. "Yes. You're right—I could have hired an actor to mimic Malcolm's voice. But, Dr. Willard, that's his handwriting. And no one else had access to all of those blood test results. But if you don't trust me, then we should go to the Broadway Bistro right now—where my friend is about to meet Malcolm. It'll just be a few minutes of your time."

Dr. Willard nodded. "Let's go."

Nancy rearranged the salt and pepper shakers on the table for what seemed like the eighth time. She was so nervous, she couldn't sit still. Malcolm was a few minutes late. If he didn't hurry up and show, then their plan would fail miserably.

She'd chosen a table in the back, so that it would be quiet enough for Dr. Willard to over-hear their conversation. Now all they needed was for Malcolm to come in and sit down, facing the wall, so that Dr. Willard could sneak in after him and sit behind him. Nancy felt as though she were staging a very elaborate play.

She sighed audibly as Malcolm entered the small café. He looked around briefly, as if to make sure no one would see him.

"Courtney, hello," Malcolm said, sitting down at the table.

"Hi, Malcolm," Nancy said. She watched Dr. Willard make his way through the crowd to the table behind them.

"Sorry I'm late," Malcolm said. "So, tell me. How did the meeting with your advisor go?"

"Fine. Just fine. He did want me to get a little more information from you, though, before I go ahead and give you a check," Nancy said.

"Okay," Malcolm said patiently. "What else did you want to know?"

"I made out the check to Revolution Drugs," Nancy said. "Is that right?"

"Yes, that's perfect," Malcolm said. "I'll for-ward it to Louis, and we can get you into the group."

"Wonderful," Nancy said. "And when did you say the drug would be approved?"

"Any day now," Malcolm said. "As long as I'm involved in the project, I'm sure we'll have no trouble getting it through."

Dr. Willard stood up. "I'm not sure how much longer you *will* be involved in the project, Malcolm," he said angrily.

"Tom! How—how nice to see you," Malcolm stammered.

"I wish I could say the same," Dr. Willard said. "Malcolm, I think we've got a problem on our hands. And that problem seems to be you."

"Me? But I haven't done anything," Malcolm protested.

"Oh, no," Ginny said, striding up behind him. "You didn't do anything at all. You only changed the lab results so your drug company could make more money."

"She's lying," Malcolm said. "She's upset because I broke it off, and—"

"We'll find out who's lying," Dr. Willard said. "But right now, it looks to me like it's you. Would you come back to my office? In fact, I'll call the hospital administrator and see if she can meet us there, too."

"Well, I'm kind of busy this afternoon," Malcolm said. "Could we make it another time?"

"No. We could not," Dr. Willard said sternly. "Come along."

Malcolm stood up and followed Dr. Willard out of the café, his head hanging. He looked defeated.

"Way to go, Courtney," Ginny said, putting her arm around Nancy's shoulders. "Hey, feel like spending any of that humongous trust fund on me? How about a frozen yogurt?"

"As soon as I go home and change. I feel like an impostor in this business suit," Nancy said with a laugh. "As though I should be in court, working on a trial!"

"For all your mental pain and suffering—not to mention your help—*I'll* treat," Ginny offered. "No lawyers—or doctors—allowed."

CHAPTER 14

Jake knocked on the door of Gail's private office, a small, glassed-in cubicle. "Hello? Gail?" She'd asked him to meet her there at three o'clock Monday afternoon to discuss a new story idea.

So why wasn't she there? He was five minutes late. He hoped she hadn't gotten ticked off at him for being late—and left. Trouble at the newspaper was just what he *didn't* need right now. He had enough problems in his personal life.

He wandered around her office, checking out framed stories on the walls.

"So you are here," Gail said, striding into her office.

"Well, I—" Jake stopped, seeing Nancy walk into the office right behind Gail.

"Wait—I thought I was meeting you, Gail," Nancy said. "To talk about a new story—"

"That's what I thought, too," Jake said. "Is this some sort of joke?"

"Have a seat, both of you," Gail instructed.

There were two chairs in front of her desk. Jake pulled one away from the other and sat down in it. Nancy dragged her chair to the opposite side of the desk and sat down.

"Now, see, this is exactly what I wanted to talk to you about," Gail said, shaking her head. "You've been doing stuff like this all week."

"Stuff like what?" Jake asked defensively.

"Like not even sitting next to each other at staff meetings. Not spending any time in the office all week—or when you were here, taking off as soon as the other person showed up. Even though you're both supposed to be developing new assignment ideas. You just keep ignoring each other—and this place," Gail said. "Look, breakups are tough. I know that. But whatever problems there are between you, you're two of my best reporters. And I need you to be able to work together here. So, figure out how. And don't come out until you do." She marched out of the office, closing the door firmly behind her.

"Subtle, isn't she?" Jake commented, glancing nervously at Nancy.

"Yeah," Nancy said. She sighed and stared up at the ceiling.

Jake drummed his fingers against the arm rests. He had a lot to get done that afternoon. He had a paper to write, a test to study for . . . He really didn't have time for this.

He looked across the room at Nancy. She seemed to be lost in thought. She probably had just as much on her mind as he did.

"The sooner we do this, the sooner we can get out of here," Jake said.

"Right," Nancy agreed.

They sat in silence a few more moments, then Jake couldn't stand the tension any longer. He took a deep breath and started to talk.

"Nancy, I'm sorry I acted like such an idiot. I mean, walking out on the meeting last week—that wasn't very mature," Jake began. He wasn't going to apologize for the reason they'd broken up. He still felt he was right about Nancy's not going out with Terry. "I should have told Gail why we couldn't do the article in the first place, instead of throwing it in your lap."

Nancy shrugged. "That's okay. I felt as weird about it as you did. I just didn't think of leaving first."

"At least she gave up on that story idea," Jake said. "That was pretty dumb, you have to admit."

Nancy finally looked at him. "We could do one called 'Best Places to Argue on Campus,'" she suggested with a sly grin.

"Hey, we could write that in our sleep," Jake agreed with a laugh.

"Jake, I'm sorry we're not so close anymore," Nancy said. "I hope we can be friends."

Jake nodded. "I think we can be. Maybe not right away, but I know we can work together."

"Good! I'm so glad you said that!" Nancy cried, jumping out of her chair. "I've been working on a story, and I could really use your help."

"No. Really?" Jake teased.

Nancy rolled her eyes at him. "It's my friend Ginny. She's volunteering at Weston General, and she found out this resident was changing lab test results—just so a drug could make it into the marketplace. I helped her turn him in. And after it was all over, I started wondering how often that happens, and I thought"—she snapped her fingers—"that's exactly the kind of investigative piece Jake and I could write together."

"I'll definitely help," Jake offered. He stood up and opened the door. "It's okay, Gail!" he called down the hall. "You can come back in now!" Then he turned around and faced Nancy. "So, want to get started on that article?"

"Ginny, I'm glad you could come in today." Dr. Mosely tapped an empty manila file folder against her desk. "I need to talk to you."

Ginny nodded. She was too nervous to talk. Ever since Dr. Mosely had called her that morning and arranged a meeting, Ginny had been hoping that she had heard the truth about Malcolm and would offer to take her back.

"I need to apologize. I should never have suspended you so abruptly. It was wrong of me to take a doctor's word over yours." Dr. Mosely sat back in her chair and put the tips of her fingers together. "We certainly know now that Malcolm's not the person we thought he was."

"Unfortunately," Ginny said.

"I've spoken with Dr. Willard. He told me you may have saved patients' lives by exposing Malcolm's fraudulent work," Dr. Mosely continued. "And we'd be honored if you'd return to the hospital."

"I'd love to come back," Ginny said.

"Great. I'm so glad," Dr. Mosely said with a sigh. "Please forgive me, Ginny. I should have listened to you."

"It's okay," Ginny said. "I mean, I was pretty upset. But if I hadn't been, I might not have been so desperate to prove Malcolm was the one who was in the wrong. So I guess everything worked out for the best."

"You can have your pick of areas to volunteer in," Dr. Mosely said. "Except the gift shop. We're covered there."

Ginny laughed. "The gift shop wasn't what I had in mind."

"Good. Because we can certainly use your

skills elsewhere," Dr. Mosely said. "Would you like to go back to research? Or to internal medicine? Neurology?"

"Sure, I—" Ginny was interrupted by a loud knock on the door.

Dr. Willard walked in. "Ah! Both of you at once. This makes my news even more pleasant."

"What is it?" Dr. Mosely asked.

"All the evidence against Malcolm has been turned over to the state medical board and the police," Dr. Willard announced. "He's been suspended from the hospital as of today, pending an investigation. But I have a feeling he won't be back—at this hospital or any other."

"And what about the medical monitors?" Ginny asked. "Were they the real thing?"

"Yes. The venerable doctors Lanter, Hardigg, and Smith," Dr. Willard said. "Malcolm paid them to make the occasional appearance at the lab and then look the other way. They'll probably lose their licenses as well."

Ginny smiled, grateful for the news. Anyone who fooled around with other people's lives didn't deserve to practice medicine.

"Thanks again for your help," Dr. Willard said. "I've got an hour before my next bypass. Can I give you a quick tour of the cardiology wing?"

"I'd love that," Ginny said, standing up to join him. "It's nice to be back."

* * *

"Leaving so soon?" Bess walked into her room after her last class on Monday and tossed her backpack onto her bed.

Ned was crouched over his duffel, packing it once again. "I might as well transfer here, at this point."

"Did they figure out what was wrong with your car?" Bess asked.

"Yeah. It cost a couple hundred, but I'm trying to forget about that part." Ned wrinkled his nose.

"Ouch," Bess said. "So you're hitting the road?"

"I have to," Ned said. "I missed an entire day of classes. I've got to get back and catch up."

"Okay. Have a safe trip," Bess said. "Thanks again for coming. I really don't know how I would have gotten over Paul without you. And thanks for getting me back into the whole social scene this weekend."

"No problem." Ned came over to Bess, taking her hands in his. "And thanks for talking to me about Nancy. You helped me put her in my past, where she belongs."

"Here's to friendship," Bess said, putting her arms around Ned's shoulders.

He put his arms around her waist and gently hugged her to him.

"Hi, George. What are you up to?" Nancy asked. She was just about to leave the *Wilder*

Times office and had put in a quick call to George.

"Oh, hi, Nancy. Will's over and we're studying," George said.

"Studying? Really?" Nancy teased.

"Really. Since everything that happened last week, I fell about a hundred pages behind in European history. Or was it a hundred years. Anyway, that's what we're doing—honest," George said. "What's up with you?"

"I just had a meeting at the newspaper. I was heading back to the dorm, but I called to see if you wanted to grab a cup of coffee or something," Nancy explained. "You're busy, though, so I guess I'm forced to start studying right away instead of putting it off for an hour—"

"Call Bess. I'm sure she'd love to spend some time with you," George said.

"Spend? I think the key word here is *waste* some time," Nancy said, laughing.

"Yeah. Wish I could join you," George said.

"I think I'll just drop by her room and surprise her," Nancy told George.

"Okay. See you tomorrow," George said. "Lunch?"

"Lunch. Definitely," Nancy agreed.

She hung up the phone at her desk and walked out of the office, waving goodbye to Jake on her way. Nancy was glad they'd worked things out so that they could be friends, or at least coworkers.

She felt as if a huge weight had been lifted from her shoulders. Or maybe my heart, she thought. Closure was always good.

She was in such a good mood that she felt like skipping as she walked along the path toward Thayer. Since the argument between her and Bess Saturday morning, Nancy had felt a little uneasy about the way things stood between them. She wanted to know how Bess was doing—beyond the happy facade she'd been putting on for everyone's benefit.

Imagine that, thinking Bess and Ned were having a relationship. Nancy practically laughed out loud. She must have been really stressed from the Jake situation to get that jealous. She'd really gone off the deep end, kissing Terry in front of Ned. What exactly did she think she was accomplishing? She'd only managed to make every single person involved uncomfortable—including herself.

The next time I kiss someone, it'll count, she told herself, walking into Bess's dorm. In fact, maybe Bess can help me figure out just who that person should be. She'd spent a lot of time with Ned—she'd know whether Ned had any interest in starting things up between them again.

She walked down Bess's hall and stopped by her door. It was open slightly. Nancy peeked through the crack. "Hello? Bess?" She nudged the door open a little farther with her foot.

Nancy gasped. Bess and Ned were standing in the middle of the room with their arms wrapped around each other!

They both turned toward the door, looking as startled as deer caught in headlights. Startled—and guilty, Nancy decided. And why shouldn't they be? They'd been caught.

"Nancy, hi," Ned began. "I—"

"Nancy!" Bess cried. "Ned was just—"

"Spare me," Nancy said, her voice shaking with emotion. "Spare me your explanation this time!"

She turned and ran down the hall, tears blurring her vision as she stumbled into the stairwell. Bess and Ned—so it *was* true!

NEXT IN NANCY DREW ON CAMPUS™:

Stephanie can't seem to get her love life on track. Loving Jonathan is no problem. Staying faithful is another story. Now she thinks she's found the perfect solution: marriage—and right away. . . . Nancy tells her to go slow. But then, who is she to talk? Lately, as far as romance goes, her track record hasn't been so hot either. . . . Nancy saw it with her own eyes: Ned Nickerson, her old love, getting close with her friend Bess. Talk about betrayal! And Nancy's in no mood to forgive. But maybe handsome track star Judd Wright can at least help her forget—until their relationship takes a startling turn . . . in *Love and Betrayal*, Nancy Drew on Campus #21.

R·L·STINE'S GHOSTS OF FEAR STREET®

A MINSTREL® BOOK

Simon & Schuster Mail Order
200 Old Tappan Rd., Old Tappan, N.J. 07675
Please send me the books I have checked above. I am enclosing $_____ (please add $0.75 to cover the postage and handling for each order. Please add appropriate sales tax). Send check or money order--no cash or C.O.D.'s please. Allow up to six weeks for delivery. For purchase over $10.00 you may use VISA: card number, expiration date and customer signature must be included.

POCKET
B O O K S

Name _____

Address _____

City _____ State/Zip _____

VISA Card # _____ Exp.Date _____

Signature _____ 1180-15

Christopher Pike presents....
a frighteningly fun new series for your younger brothers and sisters!

SPOOKSVILLE

The Secret Path	53725-3/$3.50
The Howling Ghost	53726-1/$3.50
The Haunted Cave	53727-X/$3.50
Aliens in the Sky	53728-8/$3.99
The Cold People	55064-0/$3.99
The Witch's Revenge	55065-9/$3.99
The Dark Corner	55066-7/$3.99
The Little People	55067-5/$3.99
The Wishing Stone	55068-3/$3.99
The Wicked Cat	55069-1/$3.99
The Deadly Past	55072-1/$3.99
The Hidden Beast	55073-X/$3.99
The Creature in the Teacher	
	00261-9/$3.99
The Evil House	00262-7/$3.99
Invasion of the No-Ones	
	00263-5/$3.99

A MINSTREL BOOK

Simon & Schuster Mail Order
200 Old Tappan Rd., Old Tappan, N.J. 07675
Please send me the books I have checked above. I am enclosing $_____ (please add $0.75 to cover the postage and handling for each order. Please add appropriate sales tax). Send check or money order–no cash or C.O.D.'s please. Allow up to six weeks for delivery. For purchase over $10.00 you may use VISA: card number, expiration date and customer signature must be included.

POCKET BOOKS

Name _____

Address _____

City _____ State/Zip _____

VISA Card # _____ Exp.Date _____

Signature _____ 1175-11

EAU CLAIRE DISTRICT LIBRARY

Nancy Drew on Campus™

By Carolyn Keene

- ❑ 1 New Lives, New Loves   52737-1/$3.99
- ❑ 2 On Her Own   52741-X/$3.99
- ❑ 3 Don't Look Back   52744-4/$3.99
- ❑ 4 Tell Me The Truth   52745-2/$3.99
- ❑ 5 Secret Rules   52746-0/$3.99
- ❑ 6 It's Your Move   52748-7/$3.99
- ❑ 7 False Friends   52751-7/$3.99
- ❑ 8 Getting Closer   52754-1/$3.99
- ❑ 9 Broken Promises   52757-6/$3.99
- ❑ 10 Party Weekend   52758-4/$3.99
- ❑ 11 In the Name of Love   52759-2/$3.99
- ❑ 12 Just the Two of Us   52764-9/$3.99
- ❑ 13 Campus Exposures   56802-7/$3.99
- ❑ 14 Hard to Get   56803-5/$3.99
- ❑ 15 Loving and Losing   56804-3/$3.99
- ❑ 16 Going Home   56805-1/$3.99
- ❑ 17 New Beginnings   56806-X/$3.99
- ❑ 18 Keeping Secrets   56807-8/$3.99
- ❑ 19 Love On-Line   00211-2/$3.99
- ❑ 20 Jealous Feelings   00212-0/$3.99

Available from Archway Paperbacks

Simon & Schuster Mail Order
200 Old Tappan Rd., Old Tappan, N.J. 07675
Please send me the books I have checked above. I am enclosing $_____ (please add
$0.75 to cover the postage and handling for each order. Please add appropriate sales
tax). Send check or money order--no cash or C.O.D.'s please. Allow up to six weeks
for delivery. For purchase over $10.00 you may use VISA: card number, expiration
date and customer signature must be included.

POCKET
B O O K S

Name _____

Address _____

City _____ State/Zip _____

VISA Card # _____ Exp.Date _____

Signature _____

1127-17